James Albert Frye

Fables of Field and Staff

James Albert Frye

Fables of Field and Staff

ISBN/EAN: 9783744777360

Printed in Europe, USA, Canada, Australia, Japan

Cover: Foto ©Andreas Hilbeck / pixelio.de

More available books at **www.hansebooks.com**

FABLES

OF

FIELD AND STAFF

BY

JAMES ALBERT FRYE

BOSTON
THE COLONIAL COMPANY
1894

.

ROCKWELL & CHURCHILL PRESS BOSTON

TO

THE OFFICERS AND MEN

OF THE

VOLUNTEER SERVICE

PREFACE.

THE seven fables flanked by the covers of this book have to do with as many strange and wonderful happenings in the history of an infantry regiment — an infantry regiment of volunteers — in time of peace. They are seasoned abundantly, from end to end, with that which is stranger than fiction, but they differ slightly from "muster-rolls for pay," which, I am informed, one has to submit under oath.

If you are of the volunteer service, you may be trusted, I think, to catch the spirit of these stories; if you are of The Army, you may consider the tales as illustrative of the customs of a service to which your own is but distantly related; but if it is your great misfortune to be an out-and-out civilian — why, then you must take your chance with what follows, and lay no blame upon me should you find yourself on unfamiliar ground.

In another and an earlier book I related how we of The Third came to settle ourselves in our off-duty quarters up in The Battery; how Sam, the veteran gunner of a by-gone war, won his medal, our most profound respect, and a place among us second in importance only to that of the colonel commanding; how our horse, "Acme," gained for us great renown and no little wealth; how Larry, our seventh major, rose to the rank of hero; and many other odd truths concerning the Old Regiment. So it may be that, by reason of having read these things, you are no stranger to us, to our traditions, and to our easy-going ways. But even if to-day you come for the first time into our midst, you are none the less welcome — and you will find awaiting you a chair, a pipe, and a pewter mug at our long oaken table, to say nothing of an open-hearted greeting from as good a set of fellows as ever lent their names to the adornment of a regimental roster.

J. A. F.

INVENTORY.

" On hand, as per last return, seven : taken up since last return, as per inventory, seven ; viz. — "

THE MARCH

OF THE

FORTY THIEVES.

THE MARCH

OF THE

FORTY THIEVES.

T HE long, low room that we call The Battery seemed most depressingly quiet. Sam was there, to be sure, but his presence hardly counted, for he was sound-and-fast asleep in his own little box, partitioned off in the far corner.

I foraged 'round for pipe and plug-cut, lighted up, and wandered over to the book-case. There was nothing in it — nothing that I felt up to the bother of reading. I went over to the long oaken table and picked up a copy of the *Service Journal*, but it proved to be a back number, so I tossed it down again upon the disorderly pile of periodicals, and then climbed upon the cushions of the wide dormer-window, just as the rattle of wheels upon the stone flagging in the court far below shattered the stillness of the July afternoon.

A few words in a familiar voice came indistinctly up to me ; the wheels clattered again, but more faintly, as the unseen vehicle was driven out through the archway to the street beyond ; and steadily up the long stairs, flight after flight, sounded a quick, firm tread. And then the door swung wide upon its hinges, and Bones, our surgeon — Dr. Sawin, outside the service — broke into the room, with his favorite greeting : "Hello, inside! *Never mind the guard!*"

" The countersign is correct. Advance friend," said I, from number-one post on the cushions. "Likewise, the guard, being asleep, will not turn out. Come over here, and make less riot."

"Just been to see Ali Baba," explained Bones, dropping upon a chair near the window. "He'll be mended now in a week or ten days. Thought I'd run up here to glance through the papers. Sent my gig away because it's too hot to leave the horse standing."

I slipped off my coat and tossed it to the other end of the window-seat, preparatory to elevating my feet for my greater comfort.

Bones also reduced his apparel, and provided himself with smoking materials. Then, with his first few puffs, he said, reflectively, " It's funny how that ' Ali Baba ' title has been handed down from captain to captain in ' L ' company. Why, it must be more than twenty years since the day of the first ' Ali.' "

A side glance at the surgeon confirmed the impression I had received from the peculiar intonation of his voice : his hands were clasped behind his head, his long legs were draped over the arm of his chair, his eyes were half closed, and he was on the point of being talkative.

Now I, as the latest comer upon the staff, have to serve in the capacity of waste-basket, and all the older officers feel at liberty to use me at any time when they feel the need of freeing themselves of some mildewed old yarn. So I drew a long breath, gave a grunt by way of signifying that I would suffer uncomplain- ingly, and settled myself to stare vacantly out through the open casement, under the wide, striped awning, and across the broad expanse of roofs towards the green hills, far beyond the city's limits.

"Yes, it must be all of twenty years," said the surgeon, seeing that I made no effort to escape, "for it was before I'd been enticed into the service — and I've been dealing out ginger and pills to this regiment for more years than I care to remember.

"Things were different in those days: the establishment wasn't on quite the footing that it's on now. In fact, the true military spirit was at rather a low ebb, and discipline, to put it mildly, was far from rigid. So the service — even though there were good men in it then — was rather in disrepute.

"At that time one Merrowbank was captain of 'L.' He was a typical old-timer, a *milishy*-man from the word go, and a glittering example of all that a volunteer officer shouldn't be. It was a pet theory of his that the commissioned officer should be able to find stowage for just twice as much Santa Cruz product as the enlisted man could manage to put away — and he lived up to his theory most consistently. Moreover, he had a childlike faith that Providence would keep a watchful eye upon his company property, and he never allowed himself any worry about trifles like shortages in equipment.

Well, he's been out for a long time now — and it's *nihil nisi bonum*, you know — but he had a gay old company, they say.

"When the brigade went into camp that year — whatever year it was — Merrowbank took down three officers and forty men, which was a good showing, so far as strength went, for those days. But he found himself short on rifles and great-coats and any quantity of other stuff, and his implicit faith in Providence was much shaken by the discovery; so much shaken that he felt it incumbent upon him to rustle 'round a bit in his own behalf.

"So he got his non-com.'s into his tent the first night of camp, explained the nature of the emergency, and issued a G.O., to the effect that before the next morning every man in 'L' who was short of equipment must manage to make up the deficiency — how, he didn't care a coppery cent, though he'd suggest that it mightn't be a bad idea to be neighborly with the other regiments of the brigade, just to see how well off *they* might be in the matter of State property.

"Well, the non-com.'s faithfully promulgated both Merrowbank's general order and the hint that went with it, and the captain went off on a visit to each of the twenty-four tents in Line Officers' Row, and finally stowed himself away in bed with a comfortable sense of having done his best to supplement the watchful care of Providence."

"And in the morning, I suppose, he woke up to find his property complete, and the company fully armed and equipped," said I, feeling that it was time for me to give some assurance of having been listening.

" Yes, that was about the size of it, as the story goes," assented Bones, sending a big puff of smoke on its way towards the open window. "But poor Merrowbank had rather a rude awakening on that particular morning, for he was roused by a volley of sharp raps upon his tent-pole, and a good bit before reveille, too.

"As was only natural, he swore fluently, though politely, at the people outside his canvas, and desired to know what the halle-lujah they meant by stirring him up at that hour. But on recognizing the colonel's voice —Hazeltine was colonel then—he tumbled himself out of bed in two-four time; and when he had poked his head through the tent-flaps and had discovered not only the

colonel but also old General Starbuckle standing outside in the dim, gray light, he found
his ideas coming very rapidly to him, and
apologized most profusely for the warmth of
his first greeting.

"'That's all right, Captain,' said the colonel, with ominous calmness, glancing keenly
at the blinking eyes and rumpled hair framed
by the opening in the tent curtain. 'It's
very annoying, of course, to be roused at
such an unseemly hour, after a hard day —
and night! But General Starbuckle wishes
to see for himself how quickly you can turn
out your company, in heavy-marching order,
as if in response to a sudden call for special
duty. I shall take time from the present
moment.' And he sprung open the lid of
his watch, holding it up to his face to note
the exact hour.

"Merrowbank desperately plunged into his
uniform, stirred up his lieutenants, routed
out his first sergeant, and then joined his
superior officers; the sleepy men turned out,
grumbling and growling, and commenting
profanely upon the proceedings; and finally
'L' stood formed-up in its company street.

"'Very fair work, Captain,' observed Hazeltine, closing his watch with a snap, but omitting any mention of the time taken by the formation; 'very fair indeed. Now, General, at your convenience ' —

" 'What's your strength, sir?' asked old Starbuckle, glancing along the line of ill-tempered men.

" ' Three-forty, sir,' said Merrowbank, suppressing a yawn, and wishing that the old man would be done with his precious nonsense.

" 'Arms and equipments complete and in proper condition?' questioned the general, sinking his chin deeply into the upturned collar of his great-coat, and sharply eyeing his unsuspecting victim.

" ' They should be, sir,' replied the captain, catching the point of his sword in his left hand, and bending the blade into a semicircle of shining steel.

" ' H'm! Yes, they *should* be,' grunted old Starbuckle, with a tug at his white imperial, ' but I think I'll inspect. You, sir, will remain at your post. Will you accompany me, Colonel?'

" The two senior officers slowly passed down the opened ranks, making a most minute inspection of every man. The colonel had lugged out a note-book, and from time to time, at some muttered remark from the general, he would make a brief entry, grinning wickedly at each fresh line of pencilling — for he was no friend of Merrowbank's, and he found great joy in the task in which he was engaged.

"At length — just as the drowsy drummers of the regiment were turning out to beat reveille — the inspection came to an end, and the general, coming to the front of the company, said, 'Captain, you will direct your first lieutenant to report the result of reveille roll-call. I wish a word with you in your quarters.'

"Entering the captain's tent, old Starbuckle planted himself solidly upon a campstool, frowned, and said, 'You are aware, Colonel Hazeltine, how strongly I object to having companies of line organizations bear any designation other than that of regimental number and company letter: has this company any name of an unofficial nature?'

"'It used to be called the Norfolk Fencibles, I believe,' replied Hazeltine, wondering at what the brigade commander could be driving, 'and that name is sometimes used even now — on social occasions.'

"'Norfolk Fencibles, eh? Tasteful title, that — *very!*' grunted the gray-bearded old soldier. 'And you report forty men, Captain?'

"'Yes, sir: officers, three — and forty men,' said poor Merrowbank, feeling a caravan of cold shivers go travelling down his spine, for from the general's tone he felt abundantly certain that something nasty was coming next.

"'Well, from now on,' fairly snorted old Starbuckle, 'this company will be known as *The Forty Thieves!*— and with my sanction freely given. Kindly read what you have there, Colonel.'

" The colonel pawed over the leaves of his note-book. 'One rifle, marked " M, 4th,"' he began; 'two ditto, marked " C, 4th; " one ditto, marked " B, 7th; " one great-coat, with red facings' —

"'An infantryman stupid enough to rob the gunners ought to be discharged for color-blindness, if for nothing else,' interrupted the general, in the deepest disgust.

"'One ditto, with *yellow* facings; two ditto, marked' —

"'There, that'll do!' broke in Starbuckle. 'There are two more pages full of iniquity; but I haven't the patience to listen to 'em. Not a word, sir!' as poor Merrowbank desperately began an incoherent explanation; '*not a word!* It's a bad enough business as it stands — don't try to make it worse. I'll explain for your enlightenment that I took a quiet stroll around the camp last night, to observe for myself how the men were conducting themselves, and it so happened that I was just outside your tent when you were giving your non-commissioned officers instructions in petit larceny — and canvas walls are thin, *very* thin!

"'To put it into plain English, I was eavesdropping — though unintentionally — and I must apologize, of course, for the way in which I caught you off your guard. But I wish to state right here, Captain, that I can't approve of your methods, however much I may feel compelled to admire their results; and you therefore will be allowed to send in your papers immediately upon your return from this camp. I let you down easily, sir, for the sake of this regiment, which is a good one, and as a mark of my consideration for your colonel, who is trying to bring the service into efficiency and good repute.' And with this the general rose stiffly, and marched out of the tent, without bothering to bid Merrowbank a good morning.

"And that was how The Forty Thieves came into their title. The story leaked out, as such stories will, and for the rest of that camp Merrowbank was known as Ali Baba. When his papers had gone in and he had gone *out*, the nickname was handed down to the next captain of 'L'— and it will be many a long day, I fancy, before the line of Ali becomes extinct in the regiment."

"But Ali Baba wasn't *captain* of the thieves — at least, as *I* remember the original fable," I objected.

"What's that to do with it?" demanded Bones, getting up from his chair. "Haven't you been with us long enough to know that we of The Third are never tied down by precedent?"

"But all this happened long before you were in the service," I ventured. "How does it happen that you can reel it off as smoothly as if you'd been there to see and hear it?"

"Oh, I've heard the colonel tell it so often that I've got the whole lesson by heart," admitted Bones.

"Yes," I said wearily, "*and so have I!*"

The surgeon came over to the window and for a moment stood looking down into the deserted court. The sun had sunk lower, and now its rays came slantwise under the awning and through the opened sashes, to flash in dazzling brightness upon the polished blades and glittering spear-heads of the barbaric weapons clustered on the wall above the bookcase. A fly buzzed its way across the broad track of light, and Bones made a sweep at it with his big hand, but the wary little insect promptly changed direction by the right flank, gave the slip to his burly enemy, and joined a squad of his kindred deployed in open order upon the ceiling.

"Quiet, isn't it?" said the medicine-man; "quiet as an empty fizz-bottle. Never knew the old shop to be so empty at this late hour of the afternoon."

"It's July," I suggested, "and half the fellows are out of town."

Bones turned and glanced down the long room towards Sam's corner, whence at intervals came the low sound of a contented snore. "Seems something like church, eh?" he said. "We haven't the sermon, but the proper accompaniment is all here. I take it that the veteran has yielded to heat prostration. Well, I'll not bother him: I can be my own commissary. Ginger-pop and ice wouldn't be deadly in the present state of the atmosphere. What do you say?"

"I'll follow your lead," said I, rapping out the ashes from my pipe; "ginger-pop'll do for the foundation — and I can trust you to trim it up properly."

Stepping softly, the surgeon made his way into Sam's province, presently returning in triumph with two tall glasses of golden-brown nectar, crested with finely crushed ice, and faintly suggestive of old Monogram. I manœuvred a small table into position between two roomy arm-chairs, and then refilled and lighted my pipe.

"Here's fun!" said the doctor, politely nodding in my direction, and causing a perceptible ebb in the icy tide in his glass. I made haste to secure the remaining tumbler before replying, in deference to Bones' profession, "Here's hoping for an epidemic!"

"Now, speaking of The Forty Thieves," said the doctor, setting his glass back upon the table, and thereby adding another ring of moisture to the two already in evidence upon the polished wood, " I suppose the proudest day in their history was when — just hand over that pipe, will you? It seems to be drawing like a regular flue; mine's stopped."

I groaned, but handed over my pipe and rose to hunt for another one. "Now you can chatter along like an accommodation train," I said, after I had got myself finally settled, with a fresh corn-cob in one hand and my glass within easy reach of the other.

"Meaning with plenty of smoke, and frequent stops for refreshments? Precisely," said Bones. " Well, it was a great day — the day when The Forty Thieves did up All-Italy. And nobody told me about that, either: *omnia quæ vidi, quorum magna pars fui* — Latin!"

" Yes, I'm awake to the fact," said I. " You needn't construe."

"It was all of eight years back," Bones ran on, "for it was the year before Hazeltine went up to the command of the brigade. Colonel Elliott was major then, and Curtis,

who's senior major now, at that time was
captain of 'L' and reigning Ali of The Forty
Thieves.   And I? — well, I hadn't been
commissioned, but was serving out the fag-
end of my third enlistment as hospital steward.   Gad! how the roster's changed since."

"*Tempora mutantur* — Latin!" I hastened
to put in at this favorable point.   "Proceed,
you moss-grown veteran."

"Well, this was the way of it," said the
learned doctor, acknowledging by a grin
that honors were a stand-off on the score
of dead languages.   "When it came 'round
to the time for our fall field-work that year,
Hazeltine packed us aboard the cars for
Glastonbury, down on the line of the B.S.
& N.Y.

"For a wonder, the plan of operations was
not at all complicated.   The main object of
the day's work was to practise the men in
skirmishing and in the gaining of ground by
short platoon-rushes.   So when we reached
our destination, we marched out from the
village a couple of miles, and then Elliott's
battalion was detached and posted along a
stone wall and among some farm buildings,
facing a broad sweep of open meadow, while

the rest of the regiment footed it along for a mile farther, to return later in the character of bloody invaders.

"Now, up to this point everything was simple enough. But Elliott was — and, as you may have noticed, still is — a strategist of large calibre, and he'd taken the liberty of making a slight addition to the cut-and-dried plan of campaign. About a week before, he had run down to Glastonbury to look over the ground alone, and in the course of his travels he'd made some observations in regard to the lay of the land that set him to thinking. And this is what he thought:

"His four companies were to be attacked in front by the remaining eight, and in the nature of things he was fairly certain of being defeated, but he'd noted the fact that on the left of his position there was a thick growth of young timber, with an old wood-road running off into it, and on following this up he found that it made a circuit and came out into the meadow in his front, in such a way that a force marching over it would find itself eventually in rear of the right flank of the attacking party; and therefore he reasoned that he could make things very entertaining for the colonel's contingent by availing himself of this feature of the landscape, and mentally made his dispositions accordingly.

"Now, *I* ought to have been with the main body; but when Elliott's battalion detached itself I somehow got mixed up with it, and when I found out my mistake I decided to stay where I was — notwithstanding the fact that the assistant surgeon had been assigned to duty with the defence — rather than go chasing over a dusty road after the rest of the regiment. And that was where I played in luck, for if I'd been at my proper post I'd have missed my march with The Forty Thieves, and all the sport that came in at the end of it.

"Elliott had disposed his four companies in line of battle along the stone wall, but as soon as Colonel Hazeltine's troops went out of sight around a bend in the road he gave some hurried instructions to Curtis, who straightway started 'L' company off into the woods. And then Elliott came riding down the line, and caught sight of me.

"'Hello!' says he, '*you* here? We seem to be pretty heavy laden with doctors. Just you hustle along after Curtis and his Thieves; an independent column ought to have a medicine-man of its own.'

"So I saluted, and went on a jog-trot after 'L,' with my field-case bumping and banging against my hip, and " —

"And mighty sour you were at the detail!" I hazarded, getting up and going over to the mantel after a supply of matches.

"And caught up with The Thieves just after they'd got well into the bush," said Bones, without noticing my interruption. "Well, I reported to Curtis, and got orders to march either in the line of file-closers or at the rear of the column; and choosing the latter alternative, I trudged along quite contentedly, a little N.C.S. all by myself. It was a cloudy day, with just enough coolness in the air to make marching pleasant, and I thoroughly enjoyed the tramp along the leafy, grass-grown path. The boys joked and guyed each other — we were marching route-step — and once they started in on a song with a jolly, swinging refrain to it, but Curtis shut 'em up in short order, for he didn't care to have his progress too widely advertised.

" Now, Elliott had said that a march of something like three-quarters of a mile would bring us into the desired position for flanking the colonel's hostile forces, and he'd cautioned Curtis not to cover his ground in less than half an hour; so we strolled along slowly and took things easily. But when, after travelling for the best part of an hour, we had seen no signs of a clearing, why, we rather began to wonder where we were at, and wherefore. You see, we were making our way through the thickest of thick cover, there wasn't in the whole outfit such an article as a compass, and there was no sun to tell us which way our noses pointed.

" 'This begins to grow blamed ridiculous,' said Curtis, after we'd patiently footed it for about two miles and a half. 'I'm not so dead sure about our not being lost. But I've had my orders. " Follow copy if it takes you out of the window" is a good enough rule for me '—in civil life, you know, Curtis was a newspaper man — 'and so I'll heel-and-toe it over this blossoming path until we land in the middle of next week.'

" 'Hello!' he broke out a moment later, ' the advance guard begins to show signs of life!' And with that he halted the company, as the sergeant — who, with two men, had preceded the company by a hundred yards or so — came running back towards us. 'Well, sergeant, what is it? Are we in sight of land yet?'

"'I haven't *seen* anything, sir,' reported the sergeant, 'but I just heard something like shouting, and after that a few shots; not volleys, just scattering pops.'

"'The skirmishers starting in, most likely,' commented Curtis, 'though that wouldn't account for the shouting.'

"'But the sound appeared to come from our left,' went on the sergeant; 'and that seems queer.'

"'From your *left?*' repeated Curtis, breaking-off a small twig and thoughtfully chewing one end of it. 'The deuce it did! Then we've marched half 'round a circle, or else the colonel's flanked *us.* According to all the rules of the game the enemy ought to be engaged on our right. *'Tention!* Silence in the ranks!'

"We all stood motionless in our tracks, and listened intently. And sure enough, from somewhere ahead of us and to our left, there came the faint sound of a distant up-roar, and the echo of an occasional shot.

"'H'm! I'm completely twisted,' muttered Curtis, as with wrinkled brows he stood listening to the far-off racket. 'I can't seem to make it out at all. Sounds like a picnic of the Gentlemen's Sons' Chowder Club! Well, push ahead with your men, sergeant, and keep your eyes and ears well stretched. Keep quiet, and close up, there in the company!' And we took up our march again.

"'*Halt!*' commanded Curtis, in a low tone, but sharply, as we turned an abrupt corner in the path and caught sight of the sergeant standing with one hand warningly uplifted. 'Great Scott! We seem to be operating against field-works, and heavy ones too!' For across the old road, a couple of hundred yards away down the leafy vista, there loomed up before us a high, steep embankment of bright, fresh gravel, clearly outlined against the dull gray of the sky and the dark green of the foliage.

"'Now be perfectly silent, everybody; and you, Lane' — to the first lieutenant — 'take charge of the company. I'm going to look into the situation for myself,' said Curtis.

And then quickly running forward he joined the sergeant and his men, scrambled with them up the high bank, turned to the left, and disappeared behind the shrubbery.

"For perhaps ten minutes we stood waiting and listening. The noise now was distinctly audible, and I counted the reports of eleven shots before the captain's figure again came into view upon the crest of the gravel-bank. Well, he waved his arm as a signal for us to advance, and we double-timed it down the path in beautiful form, for during that halt of ours we had been growing terribly inquisitive about what was in the wind, and we were in somewhat of a hurry to find out.

"At a gesture from Curtis we halted at the foot of the slope. He had pulled out a note-book, and was scratching away in it like a crazy reporter; but finally he ripped out two or three leaves, folded them up, and sang out, 'Corporal Campbell, you're supposed to be a sprinter: you will take this note, with my compliments, to Major Elliott — and waste no seconds in doing your distance. Give your rifle and equipments to the hospital steward. On your mark — set — *go!*'

"'And now, boys,' he continued, as the

corporal, after loading me down with his im-
pedimenta, started off on his long run, 'I've
found out what's making all this row. In
the first place, it's evident that we've been
travelling the wrong road ' — it afterwards
appeared, though Elliott hadn't notified us of
the fact, that there were *two* old wood-roads,
of which we carefully had avoided the right
one — 'and I haven't the slightest idea of
where we are. But this embankment apparently is the road-bed of that branch which
the B. S. & N. Y. is building, and about a third
of a mile from us there's a howling mob of
Italians — something less than a thousand and
more than two hundred of 'em : I didn't stop
to count — laying regular siege to a shanty
in which, in all probability, they've got their
contractors cornered like rats in a trap. I
don't know anything about the cause of the
shindy — more than likely it's the old story
of overdue pay and ugly tempers — but it's a
royal rumpus, whatever started it, and if nobody's been hurt yet, somebody's bound to be
hurt soon, unless the strong arm of the law
sits down hard upon the troubled sea over
yonder.' And with this elegant example of
metaphor he stopped to catch breath.

"'Now, after a fashion, *we* are the strong arm of the law,' went on Curtis, 'and I think it's plainly our duty to sail in, and pour the oil of peace upon the raging waters. I've no orders to cover the case; I haven't any "lawful precept" from mayor or selectmen or anybody else, but — *now don't yell!* — if you'll follow me, I'll take you along to see the entertainment. All who'll volunteer to go will come to right-shoulder!'

"Up went the fifty-odd rifles in one-time-and-three-motions, and Curtis continued: 'That's the proper stuff! Now, we shall be a half-hundred against a very good-sized mob, and though we are well enough armed, we're without any ammunition except blanks. It's dollars to dimes that the bare sight of us will quiet down the ruction, but I don't care to take any chances. I've got to fit you out in *some* way — how the pretty-pink-blazes shall I do it?'

"He stood thinking for a moment, then made the company form fours — we'd been marching column-of-twos, the path being so narrow — swung the fours into line, and caused arms to be stacked. 'Now every man of you,' said he, when the men stood clear of

the stacks, 'will provide himself with ten bits
of twig, of the same diameter as a lead-pencil,
and about half the length of one. See that
the twigs are smooth and straight, so that
they'll slip cleanly into the rifle-chamber —
and, if you want to, you may sharpen one
end of 'em. *Break ranks!* — and start in on
your whittling.'

"'Aren't you afraid that those bullets will
be liable to key-hole, Captain?' sang out one
of the lieutenants, with a pleasant grin at
his own humor and the prospect of coming
trouble.

"'Can't tell,' replied Curtis cheerfully, 'at
least, until we've tried 'em. I'm all at sea
about trajectories, initial velocities, and all
that. We'll have to work out our musketry
theories as we go along. All fitted out, you
lads down there? Then fall in!'

"The company formed up, and broke
stacks; and then Curtis gave his final directions. 'Just a word more, boys: if I have
to give the command "*load!*" you will open
chamber, thrust into the bore a wooden bullet, and send home after it a blank cartridge.
You must keep muzzles elevated, or else your
projectiles will slip out. And lastly, if the

wild men whom we're going to visit should exhibit any desire to rush us, I shall order you to drop your cleaning-rods into your barrels — and we'll try the effect of harpooning 'em at short range. That's all. Fours right — *march!*' And like a small army of ants we swarmed up the sloping bank of sliding gravel, and started on our march down the railway.

" Picking up the advance guard as we went, we tramped rapidly forward, and in a very short time came in sight of the theatre of operations. Sure enough, the comedy — or, for all we then knew, the tragedy — was in full blast, for a roaring mob of swarthy Italians was surging 'round a roughly built shanty, and amusing itself by yelling, and sending an occasional stone or bullet at the closed doors and windows. Whoever was inside was lying very low indeed, for there was no response from within to the demonstrations of the attacking party, and only the lively interest shown by those outside made it appear that the place was tenanted at all.

" The rascals caught sight of us when we were about forty rods from them, and for a moment I thought that I detected signs of a stampede; but when they saw how few we were — for fifty men in column-of-fours don't make a very imposing showing — they bunched together in a devilishly ugly and suggestive sort of way, and waited for us to come up.

"We left the railway, formed line upon a level stretch of ground, moved forward a hundred yards or so, and then halted.

"'Now may heaven forgive me the sinful thought,' said Curtis, as he stood sizing up the savage rabble before him, 'but I've seven-eighths of a mind to give it to 'em where they stand! That aggregation of deviltry is *too* tempting!' But, however strong the temptation may have been, he manfully overcame it, and stepping half-a-dozen paces to the front called out, 'Is there any one among you who speaks English?'

"For answer the children of sunny Italy sent up a derisive and most provoking yell; and so Curtis, failing to obtain an interpreter from the ranks of the enemy, turned to us, with, 'Not much satisfaction to be had from them, apparently. Does anybody in the company know their lingo?'

"It seemed that our ignorance was on a par with theirs, for nobody confessed to a working knowledge of Italian. For one insane moment, to be sure, I was impelled to step out and address the offending foreigners in the ancient tongue of their native land; but to save my soul I couldn't lay hand upon anything besides *Arma virumque cano*, and "—

" Latin again, by thunder ! " I said, enthusiastically. "Ah! but you *are* up in the humanities, Bones."

" And that, you know," placidly went on the surgeon, with a nod in recognition of my admiration, " was hardly the extent of what I wished to say — though it may have been, after a fashion, apposite to the requirements of the occasion. So I let the chance to distinguish myself slip by unimproved, and stuck to my place in the file-closers.

" ' Now I *am* in a hole ! ' admitted Curtis, after this double failure in his attempt at opening the way to a parley. ' I'm stumped at this phase of the business — and blessed if I know just what card to lead next ! '

" ' Ah! you *will*, will you ? ' he growled, as three or four stones came sailing over at us. ' Well, that's cue enough for me. *Fix bayo-*

nets!' There was a metallic rattle and clash, as the fifty steel jabbing-tools were put into place for business. 'With ball cartridge — *load!'*

"'And now, in the name of the Commonwealth,' bellowed Curtis, after he had seen his men tuck away in their rifles wood enough to keep a match factory running full time for a week, 'I command ye to disperse!'

"'Skip — scatter — *vamose!'* he added by way of explanation, waving his arms like a farmer driving away mosquitoes. 'Get a move on you, and clear out, you obstinate lunatics! *Sabe? Comprenez? Understand?'*

"It seemed to me that the mob displayed symptoms of wavering: and when Curtis, in his deepest and most awe-inspiring tone, commanded, '*Aim!'* I drew a breath of relief, for I felt that when The Forty Thieves levelled their fifty rifles in one long, threatening line, a break must surely follow. But just at this critical moment the door of the shanty was flung open, and three men dashed out and went tearing off towards the woods. And *then* the break came! — though not just in the way I had anticipated. For, utterly disregarding us, the swarthy madmen, with a

wild yell of delight, sprang off in pursuit of
their escaping prey.

"It was a horrible sight — upon my soul,
a *horrible* sight! — to see the brutal fierceness
of that sudden rush. And it made me fairly
sick to think of the pounding and stabbing
and murderous kicking that surely would
follow if the mob once caught the miserable
men whom it was hunting down. I only
wish that those who frown upon the service
could have been with us then — for they
would have had an awful object-lesson in the
necessity for maintaining the military establishment, even in this enlightened land and
in these peaceful days.

"I must admit that the unexpected hide-
ousness of the whole thing threw me clean
off my balance for the moment; but Curtis
kept his head, and did his duty as he saw it
cut out for him. 'Aim waist-high!' he commanded, running to the windward flank of
the company in order to observe the effect
of the volley. '*Fire!*' And, with a report
like that of a single big cannon-cracker, The
Forty Thieves came into the game.

"I heard a chorus of outlandish yelps and
howls immediately after the volley rang out,

and, to my infinite relief and satisfaction, when the smoke drifted up and away I saw that the rabble was scattering in every direction. Five or six men were down, but whether they'd been hit or simply had tumbled over each other, I can't say, for — with the exception of one fellow — they all scrambled straightway to their feet, and pranced off to cover in a way that convinced me that their wounds, if they had any, weren't liable to be instantly fatal.

" Well, there was *my* cue. I handed to t e nearest sergeant the rifle I'd been carrying, and ran over to hold a *post mortem* — still more Latin, you'll observe — on the man that we'd bowled over. When I started towards him he seemed to be out of it, for he lay quite still; but just as I reached him he began to jabber and snarl and twist himself into bow-knots, for all the world as if he'd eaten a peck of green apples, and was undergoing the consequences. Flapping him over upon his back I began to search for his hurt, but I didn't have to make a very extended hunt, for — well, what do you suppose I found ? "

" Can't guess," said I, fishing out a bit of

ice from the bottom of my emptied glass;
" unless your man was skewered on one of
those wooden plugs."

"That's not so wide as it might be,"
laughed Bones, " for I found a stylographic
pen — yes, sir ; a *stylographic pen !* — tightly
driven into the muscles of his neck.   Regular
hypodermic injection of ink, by ginger ! *That*
proved the pen mightier than the sword,
eh ?"

"So it would seem," said I.   "But whose
pen was it ?"

"I never found out," said the surgeon.
" Whoever it was that got excited enough to
shoot it away was too much ashamed to claim
it afterwards, and I still have it.

" Well, that's nearly all the story of the
war with Italy.   We held the field until
Elliott came up with his battalion ; and later,
Hazeltine came ploughing down the railway
with the other eight companies — after which,
of course, peace reigned supreme.   I daresay
you remember the court of inquiry on Curtis,
and the newspaper discussion about the
whole business ?"

"Yes," said I, rising from my chair, after
a glance at my watch ; " and I remember

reading that Curtis came near getting into uncomfortably hot water for taking the law so calmly into his hands."

"Humph! That was all very well," said the doctor, rising and going towards the spot where he had tossed his coat. " But if those who questioned Curtis' authority to do as he did only could have seen what *I* had the privilege of seeing, they'd have chipped in to buy him a presentation sword, instead of criticising his actions so freely. Well, I must dine somewhere, I suppose, and I think your club will do me." And we slipped quietly down the stairs, leaving Sam still sleeping.

A TALE OF TWO TOWERS.

A TALE OF TWO TOWERS.

THIS tale might just as well have been christened *Under Two Flags*, for it was under two flags, and through the medium of a third one, that all the trouble worked itself out. But, since another and an earlier writer has had the bad taste to apply this desirable title to a creation frankly lacking in the first elements of that which is the truth, I am constrained, because of its unfortunate associations, to put it to one side and seek yet another — for I find myself restricted to the setting-down of none but sombre facts. And the facts in the matter are these :

One afternoon in late September it chanced that my personal affairs took me up into the twelfth story of one of the lofty office-buildings which rear themselves, crag-like, above the very fertile soil of those shadowy and nar-

row valleys, our down-town streets. What
was my exact errand is here of no conse-
quence. It is enough if I say that I was endeavoring to make a man see a certain thing
in the same light in which *I* saw it, and that,
after having failed most miserably in the attempt, I had risen to go, when he glanced
out through the window and said, " You're
up in that sort of thing: tell me, what's
going on over yonder?"

I followed the direction of his glance,
across a mile-wide wilderness of ill-assorted
roofs and chimneys, to where the great tower
of the regimental armory lifts its bulk above
the brick-and-mortar dwarfs that cluster in its
shadow. And there, upon the summit of the
topmost flanking-turret, my eye caught the
flutter of a speck of red bunting.

" That?" said I; "why, that's a signal
detachment at flag-practice. Well, I must
be going. Sorry I can't make you listen
to reason." And I went — to risk my life
in the downward rush of an express ele-
vator.

Now, that glance from the twelfth-story
window sealed my fate for the rest of the
afternoon. My good nature had been placed

under heavy strain, and the never-ending rush and racket of the swarming streets jarred so tormentingly upon my tired head that — with the blessed recklessness of the boy who cares not one darn whether school keeps or not — I consigned business to total smash, swung myself upon a passing car, and was trundled gaily along towards freedom, sunlight, and the armory.

"For Kenryck will be there," I told myself, "and I can talk to him. And my pipe will be there, and I can smoke it. And I can sit on the parapet wall, and look out over the harbor — and forget how infernally mean everything is."

And Kenryck was there. I dropped off the car, walked down to the armory, dived into the staff-room to get my pipe from its pigeon-hole in my desk, dived into the armorer's den after a bunch of matches, and then climbed up and up, flight after flight of narrow stairs, to the top of the main tower. And there, in luxurious ease, Kenryck sat in state upon a camp-stool: a note-book on his knee, a bull-dog jammed between his teeth, and his field-glasses well in play.

"Kenryck, I'm weary," I announced, as

my head emerged from the trap in the tower
roof, "and I've come to —"

"Shut up, will you, for a minute," said
Kenryck cordially. "Hi! you, up there" —
to the signalman twenty feet in the air above
us, upon the little turret — "what's that?
How's that last message? *No enemy visible
on Lexington road?* Yes, that's right. Down
flag! Rest!" Then to me, "Hullo, old
man. Pull the rest of yourself out of that
hole, and come on deck. Royal old afternoon, isn't it?"

I stepped up and out upon the tiles.
"Don't mind me in the least, Ken.," I said.
"I've not come to bother you. I'm only
here for rest and peaceful contemplation. So
go ahead with your wig-wagging, and I'll be
a non-combatant."

"Oh, you're no bother at all," said Kenryck very kindly. "It's the inquisitive ma-
niacs who ask fool questions and think it's
queer that I don't offer to teach 'em the
whole code in five minutes — *they're* the ones
that make signalling an everlasting joy."

"I suppose so," said I, taking off my hat,
to let the fresh breeze rumple its way through
my hair. "But I've stopped your game, just

the same. Wake up those flags of yours: I like to watch them waving."

"You've stopped nothing," protested Kenryck. "I'd been squinting through these glasses until my eyes ached, and I was just going to take a minute off, when you came popping up through the trap like the fairy in a pantomime."

"I'm breaking in three new men," he went on, in a lower tone. "One of 'em"—with a nod towards the turret—"I've got in the box up there: one of my sergeants has another, out on Corey Hill: and the third one's in charge of still another sergeant, over across the river, in Cambridge, on the tower of Memorial Hall. Running a three-station circuit, you see. Message starts here, goes through the hill station, and lands on top of t'other tower: *vice versa* with the answer. I'm taking it easy, you'll notice: just sitting here in the shade and keeping tabs on the Cambridge station through that embrasure. My man overhead calls off the signals from the hill: I jot 'em down: and so I can see that they tally with the original. Great system!"

"Great head!" said I: then, with an upward glance at the clean-cut face of the young soldier leaning easily against the parapet of the turret, " You've pulled in some good men, eh ? "

" Beauties, all three of 'em ! " said Kenryck enthusiastically ; " just out of college; all from the same class. Only had 'em a trifle over three months, but they've picked up the trick to a charm. Clever? Well, rather ! Just see how easily this boy handles his business." And calling out — "Attention ! Call ' B ' station " — my friend the signal officer went on with his work.

For a time, as he told off the combinations to be made, I followed the fluttering of the swiftly dipping and rising flag. But the whole thing was Sanscrit to me, and it wasn't long before I wearied of watching it. So when Kenryck, in an interval between messages, turned to me and said, "Simple enough, isn't it? Begin to catch on ? " — I answered, "Well, perhaps in about twenty years I might, but just at present the waving of a red flag conveys to me only four meanings — ' Auction,' when it's waved before a building ; ' Miss,' when it's waved across the face of a target ; ' Stop ! ' when it's waved in front of a railway train ; and ' Come ahead fast!' when it's waved in the face of an ugly bull." And having thus frankly admitted myself a rank outsider, so far as concerned the science of signalling, I gave myself over to the soothing influence of tobacco and the contemplation of my surroundings.

It has been my fortune to find many a less attractive spot than the tiled roof of our armory tower, with its encircling parapet, broken by alternate embrasure and loop-holed merlon, and with its octagonal turret at one corner, standing — like a sentry on post — in bold relief against the sky. Moreover, the sun was warm, the breeze was cool, and the combination was altogether comforting. And I speedily forgot, one after another, the petty annoyances of my down-town day.

I stepped over to the breast-high wall, rested my elbows upon the capstone, dropped my chin into my hands, and gazed out over the world. Far down in the streets below I could see the pigmy shapes of men, busily crawling to and fro in the anxious chase after money, and seeming — they and their affairs, too — so pitifully insignificant. Which caused me to reflect that it would be good that all mankind should spend an hour each

day upon a tower, to gain a better idea of the
relative size of things. And I farther was
impressed — But never mind. This is a tale
of *two* towers, and I am allowing myself to
neglect the other of the twain.

"Mother of Moses!" muttered Kenryck,
just as I had turned — after a sweeping
glance around the range of low, green hills
which, upon three sides, hem in the city — to
look out upon the harbor, with its gray-
walled forts and glistening sails, "*Mother* of
Moses! What ails the boys in Cambridge?"

"Can't tell, I'm sure," said I, looking
across the river towards the spot where the
other tower showed itself above the trees.
"I fail to see signs of anything distressful.
Time *was* when I knew what ailed the boys
in Cambridge — but that time's long gone
by! What seems to be the excitement at
the present moment?"

"That's what I want to know," said Kenryck, as the young fellow upon the turret
began to call off the signals from the second
station. "They've just sent this message —
it's being flagged over from the hill now —
'*Big trouble here! Want advice. Shall we
explain?*' Now what does that mean?"

"Ask 'em," said I promptly. "Wig-wag the information that I'm here — ready to furnish advice in car-load lots as soon as they've sent on their explanation."

"Thanks!" said my friend, with dry politeness. "I'm more than fortunate in having you with me." Then, to the man with the flag, "O.K. that last message, Millar, and add, ' *Explain.*' "

Up and down, sidewise and to the front, went the flapping square of red bunting with its core of snowy white; while Kenryck, in readiness to catch the first responsive signal, trained his glasses upon the 'cross-river station.

"Here it comes," he said, as the distant speck of color awoke to spasmodic and rapid motion. "Now we shall be given understanding. Hello! the sergeant must be doing the flagging: Orcutt couldn't send the words along at that rate of speed."

"Translate for my benefit, Ken., will you?" said I, coming over to his side. "I'm consumed by curiosity. I'll swear solemnly not to let any information fall into the hands of the enemy."

"Pick up my note-book," he answered hurriedly, without changing his position or allowing his eyes to wander for an instant from the opposite tower, "and scratch down what I give you. Ready? Well, then, start off with this: 'Man — making — fuss — at — base — of — tower.' Got that? 'Says — Orcutt — owes — him — big — money.'"

"Yes I've got it: all of it," said I, snapping a rubber band across the page as a check upon its tendency to get away from me in the fresh breeze. "Very interesting, so far. Go on, old man: give us another chapter of it. I'm waiting."

"Ease away on your chatter, can't you?" said Kenryck, a trifle earnestly. "You'll get me all balled-up in my receiving. Here, take this: 'Man's — confounded — insolent: standing — in — street: shouting — all — sorts — of — abuse — up — at — Orcutt.' There, the sergeant's stopped sending, to give us a chance to digest what we already have."

Word by word the message, unaltered by its transmission through the hands of the party at the second station, was passed down to us by the turret signalman. Something in his tone drew my attention, and I looked up at him. He was red in the face with suppressed emotion.

"Is your man Orcutt efficient with his hands?" I asked Kenryck.

"Ought to be," he replied. "He played left guard on the eleven for a couple of years."

"You'd better ask him, then," I suggested, feeling that a rare opportunity for testing the fighting capacity of the volunteer service had arrived, "why he doesn't fly down from his roost and punch the fellow's head?"

"I will!" said Kenryck promptly. And off went the question on its trip around the circuit.

The reply came quickly back: "Citizen's name is Boardman. Has policeman with him, with some sort of papers. Orcutt's willing to punch citizen, but has serious doubts about punching policeman. Says it's all mistake: doesn't owe anybody in Cambridge." All of which I carefully entered in the book, exactly as it was given to me.

"See here, Millar!" Kenryck shouted, as he caught the sound of laughter from overhead, "do *you* know anything about this business?"

"I think I do, a little — if not a good deal," admitted that young man in a choked sort of voice, grinning down at us through an embrasure. "Yes, I think I'm in a fairly good position for understanding the whole complication."

"Humph! if it's so almightily funny I fancy we'd better have more light on it," said Kenryck, with much dignity. "We'll flag over — '*Instructions coming: wait!*' — and then I'll trouble you to explain the meaning of all this foolishness."

"It's this way," said the signalman, appearing at the parapet wall, after starting Kenryck's order upon its travels: "Orcutt and I — you may have noticed it — look almost enough alike to be taken for twins, especially since he's forced out that moustache of his. And that's the key to the mystery."

"Give the key a twist, then," said Kenryck. "Proceed with your exposition."

"To continue," obediently went on the young man, "*I'm* the party for whom this Boardman is out gunning. He keeps a place where a lot of the students have club-tables, and I used to belong to a club of fellows that resorted there for nourishment — which, I may state, was not of the highest grade, though we paid a princely price for it. Well, last winter I had to be away from college for about three weeks, and I left without giving notice to Boardman. Which resulted in two claims: Boardman's, that I owed him thirty dollars for three weeks' un-eaten grub — and *mine*, that he ought to be struck by lightning for his superhuman nerve."

"Ah! I have the clue now," said Kenryck. "Come, let's get to work on straightening out things. Pick up your flag, and—"

"But that's not quite all of it," interrupted the occupant of the turret. "You see, this man Boardman isn't a pleasant person to have dealings with. He's very rough-tongued, and never sand-papers down his sentences. And the last time we argued over our differences I was so displeased by his lack of breeding that I — well, he made me hot under my collar, and I hit him just above *his*. See?"

"Oho! he's after you for assault, is he?" said Kenryck. "That's pleasant for Orcutt!"

"Yes, for assault — and battery," assented

Millar. " And I judge that it may be *very* pleasant for Orcutt. For Boardman swore that he'd get square with me some day, and I fancy — though the reports from across the river don't go much into details — that he's considerably in earnest about doing the squaring-up without any farther delay." And, in spite of the seriousness of the situation, he gave way to another fit of laughter.

" Ah, yes! " said Kenryck, frowning darkly upon his subordinate, " all this is amazingly ludicrous, isn't it? But you'll have an aching arm, just the same, before you get through with swinging that bamboo stick of yours: for we've got to flag this story over to Cambridge — and a very pretty bit of flagging it'll make! Come, we've kept the other lads long enough on pins and needles and anxious seats: we must get to work."

The message to be sent was a long one. I sat down upon Kenryck's chair, pulled out my tobacco pouch, and charged my pipe afresh, for there seemed to be nothing requiring my immediate attention. Minute slipped after minute, while Kenryck's voice kept along in steady monotone, and the bunt-

ing above our heads — whirring and flapping
in intermittent accompaniment — busily went
on with the task of changing the spoken
words into the symbols of the code.

"There, that'll keep the hill men busy for a
time," Kenryck observed, when the flag upon
the turret gave a final downward sweep and
then became still. "Phew! it was a long
pull."

"Why don't you cut your middle station
out of the circuit?" I asked. "It would
save time if you did your talking direct."

"Couldn't think of it," he replied. "These
boys are out for practical instruction, and
I'm bound to see that they get it — *all* of
'em."

"Queer mix-up, isn't it?" said I, with a
laugh. "Wish I could have seen the proceedings at the other end of the line."

"So do I," said the signal lieutenant, join-
ing in my laughter; "but I'm afraid this last
message has spoiled the fun over there.
Well, perhaps it had gone far enough."

"'B' station has finished transmitting,
sir," announced the youth above us. "Cambridge has just made 'O.K.'"

"All right," answered Kenryck, lining his

glasses upon the opposite terminal. " Now
we'll get some results."

" All ready," said I, pulling my pencil
from behind my ear and adjusting my note-
book. " Let it come."

There was an interval of waiting, but at
last the opposite tower began to talk, and, as
Kenryck passed the words to me, I spread
upon the page this remarkable entry:

" Told Boardman mistake. Says he knows
better. Also, that we're blanked liars. Orcutt very uneasy: growing insubordinate.
Proposes to smash Boardman and policeman
too. Tried to pitch loose tiles down upon
their heads. I stopped him. Tower door
locked on our side. Which prevents mur-
der. Lieutenant better come over at once."

This was cheeringly warlike. I burst into
a roar of ill-timed mirth, while Kenryck laid
down his glasses and strode back and forth
upon the roof, giving profane utterance to
his perplexity and paying no heed to the
calling-off of the signals from the hill.

I, read over my last entry in the book, and
roared again, which caused Kenryck to pause
in his tramping, glare at me, and snap out,
" Can't you let me think ? I've got to call a

halt in this business somehow — and there you sit, braying like a Himalayan donkey, and rattling the last idea out of me! How about those car-load lots of advice? Come, suggest something!"

"Heaven forbid!" said I, very earnestly. "This is your affair, and I'd never venture to hint that you're not more than able to swing it alone. You've managed it beautifully so far as you've gone. But unless you want your corps to come in for a heap of free advertising in tomorrow's papers, you'd do well to make another move — and a quick one."

"I'll call for a cab, and go over there myself," announced Kenryck, with a vicious stamp upon the tiles, "and, by The Great Indian! when I *do* get there I'll give everybody — "

"Now just hold hard for a minute, my son," I put in at this point. "Consider things calmly. What's the use of going to all that bother? Besides, it would cost you all of three large dollars — and you can't draw mileage for that kind of travelling. There's a much easier and less troublesome way out of it."

"Let's have it then!" sputtered Kenryck. "You set yourself up to be a sort of lawyer, don't you? Well, here's an elegant chance to show your quality."

"I am a lawyer," said I, with unassuming dignity; "a young but very subtle one. And since it's your wish that I should be of counsel in this case, why, I'll settle your matter very speedily for you — and at something off from my usual rates. In fact, I'll call it a charity job, and make no charge whatever. Now, pay attention to what I'm telling you. Here's what you'll do: order your sergeant to keep Orcutt quiet — if there's no more convenient method, he may tip him over and sit on him — until I can — "

" *Yes*, he may!" put in Kenryck, in a highly aggravating tone. "Why, Orcutt weighs well up towards two hundred, besides being as full of temper as a razor blade — and the sergeant's a little man!"

"Will you hear me out, you gibberer?" I inquired gently. "I don't care how you manage it, but I want you to see to it that matters are kept *in statu quo*, until I come back. Understand? I'll be gone only a minute." And I gracefully lowered myself through the trap, and went rattling down the many flights of stairs that twist their way up through the tower's dusky interior.

By rare good fortune I reached the ground floor without breakage of bones, and straightway made for the staff-room, where I hastily rummaged through my desk until I came upon a thin, black volume, emblazoned with the arms of the State, and inscribed in golden letters, "Militia Law." Hastily running over its pages I found what I needed: and then, turning down the leaf, I thrust the book into my pocket, and started off for my second ascent into mid-air.

"Here you are, Ken.," I cried, as I scrambled breathless out upon the roof. "I've brought you a bomb, and you can chuck it over into Cambridge as soon as you please."

"You've been long enough in getting it," was his ungracious response. "It wouldn't take more than five or six of your 'minutes' to make an hour. Come, trot out your alleged bomb. Time's precious."

Withering Kenryck with a single expressive glance, I slowly drew out my little black book, opened it at the marked place, and said, "It would be serving you no more than properly, you ungrateful beggar, if I should draw out of this case altogether, and leave you up the tree! I may have taken a few seconds over a minute, but I'm willing to give plump odds that — going and coming — I've made a new regimental record in tower climbing. Well, here's the medicine for your man Boardman — "

"You must excuse me, old chap," said Kenryck hurriedly. "I dare say you tobogganed down on the banisters, and galloped up again on all-fours — but you certainly seemed a devil of a time in doing it."

"Chapter three-sixty-seven, section one-nineteen, of the Revised Statutes," I began, after receiving this graceful and ample apology, "would seem to furnish both the authority and the means for the abatement of this nuisance of which you make complaint. It runneth thuswise: 'If any person interrupts or molests or insults, by abusive words or behavior, or obstructs any officer or soldier while on duty or at any parade or drill, he may be put immediately under guard and kept at the discretion of the commanding officer of the detachment until the duty is concluded: and such commanding officer may

turn over such person to any police officer or
constable of the city or town : and said police
officer or constable shall detain him in custody for examination and trial : and any person found guilty of either of the offences
enumerated in this section shall be punished
by imprisonment in the jail or house of cor-
rection not exceeding six months, or by fine
not exceeding one hundred dollars.' "

I flatter myself that I must have read this
tangle of clauses with truly judicial emphasis
and solemnity, for — when I came to the end
of it, and demanded, " How's that?" —
Kenryck gave a yell of delight, and shouted,
" Out at the plate, by Jupiter !" And the
youth upon the turret displayed such violent
symptoms of joy that I feared lest he should
tumble from his dizzy perch.

" Oh! that's too good to be true," gasped
Kenryck, after a prolonged paroxysm of
laughter. " It fits like an old glove, too !
Well, here goes for trying it on : I'll send
over the whole blessed section, though it'll
make an outrageously long message, and
order the sergeant to spout it down at 'em
from the tower. Jumping Jonah ! *won't* it do
'em up ? "

"It's a beautiful bit of rhetoric," said I, glancing through the passage again; "there are just twelve *or's* in it — enough to fit out a 'varsity eight and two single scullers. But I consider that it will answer your purpose very cleverly."

I handed over the book, pointed out the all-powerful section, and sat down, more than well pleased with my share in the proceedings. Kenryck explored the interior of his braided blouse, discovered a cigar, and silently handed it to me — an action which proclaimed more eloquently than words his deep appreciation of the value of my services.

The transmission of this lengthy quotation from the law of the land took some little time. My cigar burned slowly on until half its original bulk had fallen away in ashes before we caught the first signal in reply to our communication. But the response, when finally it came, made us speedily forget the time we had spent in awaiting it.

"Stand by to register," cautioned Kenryck, who for several minutes of silence had been sharply scanning the far-off tower. I hurriedly drew out my knife, and put a better point upon my pencil. "There she blows! Ready are you? Then score up this —

"'Have quoted law. No go! Boardman says law may be dash-double-blanked, and men who made it may be blank-double-dashed. Policeman says law doesn't concern him : his orders are to arrest on warrant. Big crowd gathered in street, guying us. Situation something awful. Orcutt in open mutiny. Will Lieutenant *please* come?'"

This was sufficiently definite, surely. Kenryck turned and stared blankly at me. Out of respect for his feelings I refrained from laughing.

"When you get that message from the hill," he shouted to the man upon the turret, "make your acknowledgment signal, and then send over word that I'm coming. Can you do it alone?" And, upon receiving an affirmative answer, he made for the trap in the roof and disappeared.

I hastily stuffed the note-book into my pocket, and followed him. Down the shaking stairs we went, at a neck-or-nothing pace, until we landed at the bottom. And then Kenryck shot himself into the armorer's room, and dropped into the chair before the telephone.

Br-r-r-r! went the little bell. "Hello! Central? Give me Cambridge, please." A pause. "This Cambridge? Well, will you give me the chief of police?" Another and a longer wait. "Hello! You the chief of Cambridge police? I'm Kenryck — Lieutenant Kenryck — commanding signal corps, third volunteer brigade. Got that? *Yes!* Well, I've sent a detail over to Memorial Hall, under duty orders. Now, my men are being interfered with and insulted by a citizen. There's a curious sort of mistake." Here he put in an elaborate explanation. "But the thing must be stopped, right away. I make formal complaint to you, under section — wait a second, please."

I supplied him with chapter and verse for the text of his discourse, and he went on, "Under section one-nineteen, chapter three-sixty-seven, of the statutes. And I want you to take this citizen — *yes,* Boardman's his name, but I don't know the initials — into custody until I can come over to attend to him. What's that? You'd like to look up the statute? All right — only kindly be quick about it."

Then came a long interval. I ventured to

say a word or two, but Kenryck turned upon me a warning scowl which reduced me at once to silence. "Hello!" he finally sang out, in answer to some communication over the wire. "You'll see that your men take care of him? That's good. Thanks! Hope we may be able to do as much for *you*, some day. I'll be over later. Good day."

He hung the receiver upon its hook, rang off, and rose from his seat, smiling like one who feels conscious of having done a clever thing. "It's a poor law," said he, "that can't be worked both ways."

"Yes, the law may be likened unto a double-edgéd sword—and woe upon them that monkey therewith!" I replied. "And now what?"

"Now we'll scale the tower again," announced Kenryck, "to await developments. And, unless I'm wide in my guess, we'll find things running *our* way when we get our next news from over the river."

"You're not going over, then?" I asked.

"No," said Kenryck very decĭdedly; "not if I know myself. It would cost me all of three large dollars—and one can't draw mileage for that sort of travelling." By which I was led to believe that a part, at least, of my advice had not fallen upon stony ground.

"I shall let the police gather in my man," he went on, as we panted up the last steep flight of stairs, "and then, after the siege has been raised, telephone over that I'll not press the charge against him. How'll that do?"

We climbed out, one after the other, upon the roof. Kenryck in a few words explained to his signalman what had been done, and then we sat down to await the final report. It was not a long waiting. In less than ten minutes the bit of color upon the Cambridge tower began its weird dance and, signal by signal, industriously sent across to us these tidings of comfort and joy:

"Patrol wagon just sailed up! Boardman bundled into it, speechless with rage. Policeman gone, too. Crowd has applauded operations and mostly dispersed. Orcutt manageable again — and coast clear."

I shook hands with Kenryck. The youth upon the turret — who, without waiting for the hill station to repeat, had translated all this for his own benefit — waved his flag madly 'round his head, and then hugged himself with delight. And we all three roared in chorus and loudly.

" We'll let it go at that," said Kenryck finally, "and call it a day's work. Make your signal for closing stations, Millar, and pack up your kit. Here," as he happened to look in my direction, " you can't have those ! "

" Oh, yes, I can," said I, folding up and stowing away in my pocket the two leaves that I had just torn from the note-book. " Of course I can have 'em. Aren't they in my own handwriting ? And besides, they'll be useful — labelled 'Exhibits *A* and *B* ' — when I'm retained to defend you against a suit for false imprisonment."

But the suit has never been brought, and the stolen leaves lie undisturbed, pasted side by side in the big scrap-book which rests upon the top of the book-case, up in The Battery. Ask Sam to hunt them out for you, when next you happen to find yourself up there.

ONE FROM THE VETERAN.

ONE FROM THE VETERAN.

"EVERYTHING'S calm," said the lieu-tenant-colonel, "and apparently lia-ble to stay so. I've been through the whole brigade — 'way down to the cavalry quarters, and back through the gunners' and infantry camps — and the peacefulness of things reminds me of the old nursery jingle,

> 'And all through the house
> Not a creature was stirring,
> Not even a mouse.'

Well, this tour of mine's been an easy one. I've been under canvas with the old brigade for just nineteen rolling years, and so when I say that this camp walks right away with the trophy for quietness, I'm speaking by the card."

"Wouldn't it be a pious idea if we were

to turn in, then?" inquired the adjutant, adding to his remark a suggestive and very audible yawn. "Field officers of the day aren't supposed to sit up all night — at least, not in time of peace. I'm feeling just a wee bit sleepy myself."

Midnight had come and gone. The camp lay silent, its snowy tents looming out dimly in the faint, midsummer starlight. Not a murmur hinted at the presence of the three thousand sleeping men hidden away beneath the shimmering whiteness of the canvas. The sleepy sentry pacing slowly to and fro before regimental headquarters seemed only a deeper shade in the shadowy picture. His measured tread upon the dew-dampened turf roused no echo.

There came into view a spectral shape, striding rapidly towards the quarters of the non-commissioned staff. "Hi!" called the lieutenant-colonel softly. "*Hi!* that you, Sam?"

At this challenge the spectre changed its course and approached the adjutant's tent, in front of which, and under the protecting fly, the two officers were sitting. "Yes, it's me," answered the voice of the veteran orderly of

The Third. " That you, Col'n'l Wentworth?
Anything I can do for ye ? "

" I'd be glad to know why you're prowl-
ing 'round at this time of night," said the
lieutenant-colonel mildly. " You're old
enough to be setting the boys a better example."

" I judge ye're correct, Col'n'l," assented
Sam, still standing attention in front of the
tent. " I'd oughter be in quarters. But
down in B Comp'ny's street I run'd onto a
feller that was in the war. Now, them fellers
is gittin' scarcer'n honest men in the city
gov'nment, an' so it follered that we got to
yarnin', give an' take, turn an' turn about,
'til we clean lost track o' the time."

It might be well to mention here that Sam
is *the* privileged character of the Third Infantry. It has been explained elsewhere how
Colonel Elliott discovered the old man enjoy-
ing his well-earned *otium cum dig.* in the
Soldiers' Home, down at Old Point. It also
has been told how, by a risky bit of work,
back in '64, he won the Medal of Honor which
he wears upon the breast of his dress-coat.
To be sure, he guesses, " Bein' nothin' but
copper, 'taint worth much " — but by the rest

of the Old Regiment it is held at a somewhat
higher valuation.

Now, the customs of The Third do not
tend to encourage the spinning of yarns by
enlisted men in officers' quarters, but to this
well-established rule there is one exception.
That exception is made in favor of Sam. And
since his webs of fact and fancy are woven,
for the most part, after darkness has de-
scended upon the face of the earth, the breach
of service etiquette is not sufficiently evident
to be demoralizing. All of which is explan-
atory.

The adjutant stepped back into the depths
of his tent, and presently returned with a
fistful of cigars and an extra camp-stool.
"Set ye, Sam," said he, appropriating one of
the veteran's pet idioms. "Set ye, and lend
a hand at smudging out mosquitoes."

The old orderly borrowed a light from the
lieutenant-colonel, and seated himself, with
his elbows resting upon his knees and his
hands comfortably clasped before him. "I've
bin a-thinkin'," said he, "how this milishy
business has changed since I was a boy.
Never happened to see an ol'-fashioned muster, did ye? Nat'rally not. Ah, them was

the days o' plumes an' swords, an' ginger-bread an' rum, an' *genuine* patriotism ! "

The adjutant, forgetting the darkness, winked at the lieutenant-colonel. Wentworth rose, stepped outside for a final survey of the sleeping-camp, and then returned to his place. " There were giants in those days, eh ? " he said, turning up the collar of his great-coat.

" Yes, ther' was," said Sam, impressively, " ther' was indeed. An' giant-killers, too. Ol' Col'n'l Leatherbee was a giant. You'd oughter seen *him !* Six-foot-two, he was. My land ! he was a rare sight when he was in his milishy togs, with his boots an' spurs, an' his buff breeches, an' his blue coat with buff facin's, an' his flamin' red sash, an' his terru-ble long sword, an' his high shako, with the wavin' plume a-top an' the soarin' brass eagle on the front of it." Sam paused for lack of breath.

" An' Maj'r Otis Prouty was another giant," he continued. " I've told ye how the Maj'r trounced ol' Col'n'l Leatherbee, up to Lond'n-derry muster. No ? Oh, that was a tremen-jous battle," he chuckled softly to himself, " a tremenjous battle while it lasted."

" *So ?* " queried the adjutant. " Was it

the custom for junior field-officers to thump their chiefs ? ”

“ Gen’rally, no,” said Sam.   “ As a rule ’twa’nt a safe undertakin’, ’cause the men that rose up to be col’n’ls was men that run’d to pritty large sizes. Ol’ Leatherbee was a man o’ consid’able breadth an’ heft. But he was some lackin’ in sperrit. O-ho ! he cert’nly *was* lackin’ o’ gimp. An’ the time when Otis Prouty tipped him over was only one o’ two times that he was downed with all four p’ints a-touchin’. For ther’ was another time ’sides that ’un.”   And here the old gunner again laughed softly over some remembrance.

“ I guess I’ll have to tell ye. ’Twas like this : the ol’ Col’n’l, a’ter runnin’ in single harness for nigh onto fifty year, had to go an’ git himself married. Not that ’twa’n’t right for him to do’t ; the Scriptures has established the principle that ’taint well for man to be alone. Only, mistakes sometimes happens. An’ Col’n’l Leatherbee added one more mistake to the list when he went an’ had himself mattermonially yoked with Tildy Pettus. By doin’ which he shown the beauty o’ the tex’ which states that fools goes a-rushin’ in where angels is ’fraid o’ bein’ entertained unawares.

"I said, didn't I, that ol' Leatherbee was a giant? Wal, Tildy, *she* was a giant-killer! 'Fore she was promoted to the command o' the Col'n'l's establishment she used to be a school-ma'am. An' if she didn't rule her little, red-painted institution o' learnin' with a rod of iron 'twas only 'cause birch-rods come cheaper an' handier, besides bein', when sci'ntifically applied to youthful students, more blisterin' than iron in a highly-het condition. Oh, she made a great name for herself as a discipliner, an' when she quit teachin', the boys an' girls o' that time felt that life still had some sweetness left for the downtrodden an' oppressed. They likewise made existence a burnin' torment for the nex' teacher, which happened to be a dyspepsic striplin' from somewheres down-country.

"Now, Tildy Pettus — I mean Mis' Col'n'l Leatherbee — were 'thout doubt a good looker. She wa'n't tall; the ol' Col'n'l useter say, 'She aint long for this world ' — meanin' that she stood 'bout five-foot-three in her high-heeled slippers. Her cheeks was quite red an' attractive, an' she was plump an' wholesome to the eye. But ther' useter be a kind o' furrow that'd crease itself down 'twixt her

eyebrows when things didn't go just to suit
her, an' when that occurred, which wa'n't un-
frequent, them that knew her took it for a
sign that 'twas 'bout time to display the
better part o' valor — which, so we're told, is
discretion. For Tildy had a tongue — a *sharp*
'un — an' a copious dictionary to draw words
from when the sperrit moved her to the usin'
on 'em.

"Not that, in speakin' o' the sharpness o'
the female tongue, I'm castin' any reflections
on wimmin-kind *as* such," explained Sam.
"Lor' knows I've been admirin' wimmin more
or less for better'n half a century. But some
on 'em, havin' tongues o' great keenness,
makes remarks which cuts most distressful.
An' yet, if female tongues be keen, the male
tongue often is blunt ; an' I haint yet quite
made up my mind whether it hurts the worst to
be cut by a sharp tongue or bruised black-an'-
blue by a blunt 'un. It's some'at a'ter the
fashion o' politics — ' Both the Old Parties
has grave defec's in their make-up.'

"Wal, Mis' Leatherbee settled down as
commandin' officer o' the big, white house
wherein the Col'n'l hitherto had reigned
alone, in fancy meditatin' free. An' lackin'

her former exercise o' disciplinin' scholars, an' havin' no childern of her own to put through a course o' sprouts, she fell into the way o' providin' herself with amusement by a-teachin' her husband of his P's an' Q's. An' this was very entertainin' for the both on 'em. For she'd bin used to seein' her dear little pupils set up an' take notice when she spoke to 'em; while the Col'n'l — wal, he'd bin accustomed to doin' pritty much whatever he darn' pleased, an' furthermore had got well sot in the habit. However, like most men that gits married late in life, he was fond of his wife, an' when she didn't go for to nag him too hard they managed to jolt along together well's most married folks.

"Now, one o' the Col'n'l's pet habits, I must tell ye, was to employ a consid'able share of his evenin's, durin' the winter, in settin' into a congenial cotery which was in the way o' gatherin' themselves together 'round the fire-place at the ta-avern. He were a man o' some prom'nence in them parts, an' what he said carried great weight, he havin' bin to the legislatur' for a couple o' terms, an' havin' bin selec'man time out o' mind, 'sides havin' held 'most every title in

the milishy 'ceptin' jigadier-brindle — which
is what the boys useter call the briga-
dier gen'ral. So his remarks nat'rally was
received with great respec', an' when he
explained the strategematical mistakes that
was made by both sides durin' the Revolu-
tion an' the War of 1812, ther' wa'n't no
one that felt called upon to set up a very
vehement opinion to the contrariwise. 'Specially while he was a-settin' up o' the rum,
which, for to give him his dues, he done as a
rule, an' freely ; sometimes so freely that
when it come breakin'-up time, both him an'
his constituents would be a-showin' sympt'ms
o' coagulation o' the speech.

"From all o' which it follers that in some
ways ol' Leatherbee was the darn'est man ye
ever seen. Which bein' so, his wife must o'
necess'ty bin the nex' to the darn'est. In the
ı.--ʻ place, 'twa'n't proper nor 'cordin' to the
rules o' polite behavior for him, havin' satu-
rated his system with ol' Santy Crooze ex-
tracts, to go home an' try to convince Mis'
Leatherbee that, if he'd bin in command o'
the American forces, the maraudin' British
wouldn't never've had occasion to make a
hollowcost o' the city o' Washin'ton ; because

she, not bein' a soldier, couldn't be expected
to take no int'rest in topics o' them kind,
'specially at the untimely hour o' night at
which they usually was brought up for her
consid'ration. *And* which bein' all granted,
'twa'n't, in the second place, hardly good taste
on her part to address such remarks to her
errin' spouse as she sometimes allowed herself for to do; 'cause, if he wa'n't her superior,
he cert'nly was her senior. An' no man o'
proper respec' for himself enjoys bein' called,
earnest-like, a 'sozzlin' soak.' This ye may
set down for a fac', sure's ye're a foot high.

"P'raps I'm goin' too heavy into details,
an' not figgerin' my account down to a p'int
fine enough to match the lateness o' the
hour. But I've told ye enough, anyways,
to make it evident that the affairs o' the
Leatherbee household was runnin' along in
a fashion that was bound to wind up in a
climax sometime. An' finally the climax
come, the arrival of it bein' somewhat in
thiswise:

"'Twas on a terruble stormy night, 'long
towards the end o' Jan'ary. The ol' Col'n'l
had went down to the ta-avern uncommon
early, an' had evened things up by stayin'

more'n respectable late. So when he fin'lly got himself boosted out'n his chair by the fire, an' started off to go home, clean to t'other end o' the town, the clock in the steeple o' the Orthodox church had got through with the business o' knockin' out midnight an' was a-puttin' up its hands to strike the next hour which might happen to come along that way, feelin' confident, as ye might say, that it could send it to sleep in one round.

' " 'Col'n'l,' says the ol' man to himself, as he went ploughin' along through the snow, 'Col'n'l, ye have tarried too long with the serpint which do lurk in the wine-cup.' This, however, wa'n't stric'ly true, 'cause ther' hadn't bin no wine at all connected with the evenin's entertainment, he havin' confined his attention exclusive to rum-an'-molasses.

" 'Col'n'l Leatherbee,' says he again, a little further on, 'I've sore misgivin's in regards to the reception that's a-waitin' ye yonder.' It was a great trick o' the ol' man's to talk to himself when a-laborin' under stimulous excitement. But he always done it respectful, never allowin' himself to

forgit the position in the community which
he held. At the proper time an' place he
was able an' willin' to swear the legs off'n
an iron pot; but he never swore at himself, nor at his wife, neither.

"'I must be firm in the hour of adversity,'
says he, when he had steered himself far's
his own gate. '"Budge not, lest ye be
budged" shall be my motter. I will be
silent under the wrath to come. It is written that strong waters run deep; *I* will run
deep also.' This is what he actu'lly said. I
know it, because the ol' man had bin talkin'
in a very deep tone, so's to give himself all
the courage possible, an' the lan'lord o' the
ta-avern heard every blessed word, he havin' follered the Col'n'l far's his door, to make
sure that he didn't lay himself down to slum-
ber in no snow-drift, arguin' that he were too
valuable a customer to be careless of.

"Wal, Col'n'l Leatherbee navigated careful acrost the door-yard, leavin' a trail as
crooked as if't had bin made by the serpint
which he'd mentioned, but the beautiful
snow come down an' covered the tracks,
so's they shouldn't set the neighbors to talkin' next mornin'. An' that was the last

seen o' the Col'n'l, that night, by any mortal
eye 'ceptin' his wife's. However, the rest
o' what I'm goin' to tell ye sets on a pritty
good foundation, for it comes direc' from
Mis' Leatherbee herself, she havin' bin so
tickled by the subsequence of events that
she just couldn't keep her mouth shet, an'
had to go trottin' over to tell the whole
story to her nex' best friend. By which
channels the report was duly an' officially
promulgated.

"After wrastlin' successful with the latch
o' the door, the ol' man ushered himself into
the house. An' then, havin' pulled off his
boots an' dumped his big coat, snow an' all,
down onto the floor, he slipped into the
sleepin'-room an' begun to diverge himself
from the rest of his clothin'. Everythin'
went fust-rate for a while, not a whisper
comin' from the big four-posted bedstid to
disturb his nerves. But Mis' Leatherbee
was just layin' low, like a masked batt'ry.
An' all of a sudden she opened onto him.

"My gor-*ri!* She begun with solid shot,
an' then changed off onto percussion shell,
an' fin'lly started a-servin' out canister. The
tempest outside had bin doin' tol'able lively

work up to this p'int; but when Mis' Leatherbee got fairly het up to the occasion the
wind give a last despairin' howl, an' went
switchin' down the valley an' into the nex'
township, like it owned up that it wa'n't runnin' no opposition to the rumpus she was
a-raisin.'

"The ol' Col'n'l, he were took completely
by su'prise, bein', as it were, off'n his guard.
He'd bin expectin' a to-do o' some sort, but
the rakin' he was a-gettin' went clean beyond
his most cheerful calculations. For a minute
he stood stock an' still in his tracks, plumb
dumb-foundered. An' then his knees got
wobbly, an' he sot down suddin on the floor,
for to collec' his idees.

"So far it had bin a jug-handled discussion — meanin' that all the talkin' had bin
on one side. An' as the ol' man sot ther' a-
rummagin' for thoughts, he come acrost his
original plan, layin' tucked away safe an'
sound under the roof of his head, an' recol-
lected that he wa'n't a-goin' to say nothin',
no matter what happened.

"But, 'stid of abatin', the roarin' whirl-
wind of abuse kep' growin' stronger, an' the
Col'n'l kind o' lost sight " —

"*S-st!*" broke in the adjutant, raising his hand, and leaning forward. "Hear anything?"

"Yes; sabres a-clinkin'," answered Sam promptly, cocking his head to one side and peering out into the gloom. "Ye can't fool me on that sound; I've heard it too often, farther south than we be now. Guess likely it's the provo's."

The lieutenant-colonel stepped out from beneath the tent-fly, and went to meet a little squad which was making its way up from the left of the line. After a moment's parley he returned to the tent, and the shadowy group moved on, the clank of the sabres sounding more faintly as the troopers vanished into the darkness. "Two of the provost-guard, running in a tramp found asleep back of the cavalry stables," he explained, as he seated himself. "Proceed with your fiction, Sam."

"Queer, how them tramps always hang 'round volunteer camps, aint it?" said Sam. "Ther' aint nothin' in it for 'em, 'ceptin' the guard-house if they happens to git collared. An' yit they turn up reg'lar, year in an' year out. Must be they're sent providentially for to give practice to the provo's. Le' me

see ; where was I ?   O, yes ; ye left we two
a-settin' here, an' ol' Col'n'l Leatherbee a-
settin' on the floor of his bedroom, waitin' for
the clouds to roll by.   Wal, I'll proceed, but
not with no fiction ; what I'm given' ye is
solemn an' sacred fac's.

"The clouds in the Leatherbee mansion,
'stid o' rollin' by, kep' growin' heavier an'
blacker, an' Mis' Leatherbee's stock of ammunition didn't show no signs o' runnin' low.
So fin'lly the ol' Col'n'l's dander begun to
come up, an' 'fore he knew it, he'd forgot
that he were goin' to suffer all things in un-
complainin' silence.

"'Mis' Leatherbee,' says he, 'my dear
mad'm, like the wintry snow, we are driftin'
— *hic!* — driftin' apart.   At the present moment we're as far apart's the two ends of a
stick.   Which means bein' sep'rated as widely's the feeble human intellec' can conceive.'
Now, anybody with eleven idees to the inch
might have seen that the ol' man wa'n't in no
condition to pass remarks with his good lady ;
but, oncet havin' got fair started, he progressed
right along, regardless o' the fac' that he were
violatin' the agreement he'd made with himself previous.

" " 'Tis best that we should end this pain-
ful interview,' he says, a-climbin' up onto
his mutinous legs. 'Alas! ther' aint but one
way, an' that a awful — *hic!* — awful gashly
one! But ye've drove me to't. I ther'fore
bid ye farewell, Mis' Leatherbee. I also trust
that your few remainin' years may be cheered
by no remorse. Your very respectful an'
obedient servant, Nathan Leatherbee, Col'n'l
commandin' Tenth Reg'ment Milishy.' This
may sound ridic'lous, but it's word for word
what the ol' man said. Honest! His brain
was so shooken-up by the razzlin' he'd bin
gittin' that he truly couldn't tell whether he
were makin' of a speech or writin' of an
official letter.

" Wal, bein' more or less firm established
on his feet, he zig-zagged himself out into the
kitchen, his house follerin' the plan o' most
country houses o' that time, an' havin' a
thunderin' big kitchen, with a lot o' rooms
openin' out of it. Here he sashayed over to
the cupb'd, an' took out a slashin' big carvin'
knife, an' begun to whet it up on the steel
which went with it, makin' more noise than
a hay-maker puttin' an edge onto his scythe.
Mis' Leatherbee had stopped talkin', an'

'twas plain to be seen that she were a-listen-
in' to the proceedin's.

" The ol' Col'n'l fixed the knife to suit him,
an' then slipped into the closet an' fetched
out a ham which happened to be there, settin'
it down careful-like onto the table. 'Mis'
Leatherbee, do ye relent?' says he in a solemn tone. If she did, she didn't say so.
' Ther's yet time, ma'am,' says he, pausin' for
a reply. Not a word come from the bedroom; the silence was truly appallin'.
' Once more, then,' says he, in a chokin'
voice, ' an' for the last time, farewell !' An',
with that, he plunked the carvin' knife into
the ham, with a sick'nin' *chug*, give a fearful
groan, an' flopped down heavy onto the
floor.

"Now, 'twas gol-*dum* cold out ther' in the
kitchin, an', as I told ye, the Col'n'l had dis-
pensed with most of his clothin' before bein'
drove to the committin' of his rash deed.
Consequently, after layin' ther' in the dark
for a minute, he begun to have chills, an', to
keep his teeth from chatterin', he had to
groan some more, which he done this time in
good earnest. But Mis' Leatherbee staid
comfortable in bed.

"Wal, fin'lly Col'n'l Leatherbee give a combination o' groan an' gasp an' guggle that fair rattled the dishes on the closet shelves. An' then his wife speaks up, an' says, says she, ' Aint ye dead yet, *Mister* Leatherbee ?' To which he answered, truthful, 'No; but I'm tormented nigh to bein' !' — 'Hurry up an' die, then,' says she, 'I want to be gittin' to sleep.' An' he heard her turnin' over in bed, an' smoothin' down her piller.

"That was the last straw that done the giant-killin' business. The ol' man riz up slow, leavin' the murdered ham layin' in its gore on the table, an' sneaked back into the bedroom, an' crawled in under the quilts, feelin' smaller'n a cent's worth o' soap a'ter a week's hard washin'. An', for oncet in her life, Mis' Leatherbee had sense enough to hold her raspin' tongue, an' let her husband go to sleep in peace."

"Here comes the relief," said the lieutenant-colonel, as the sentinel at headquarters advanced to meet an approaching knot of men, and sharply challenged, " *Halt! Who's there ?* "

"Whew! then it's two o'clock," said Sam, hastily rising. " Who'd have thought it? This aint no sort o' way for a man o' my age to be a-keepin' his roses fresh."

"Any moral in all that?" asked the adjutant, rising in his turn.

"No; nor nothin' un-moral, neither," chuckled the veteran, raising his hand to his cap in parting salute. "Which, in these days, is good guarantee that 'twont never be printed. Wal, good-night to ye."

WOODLEIGH, Q.M.

WOODLEIGH, Q.M.

MOST of us have cause for remember-
ing the hospitalities of The Fourth.
The same being an up-country regiment, a visit to it involves a rail journey of
three hours and thirty times as many miles;
but, in view of what lies at the end of them,
the ninety miles and the three hours count
as nothing. For in The Fourth they know
how to do things properly.

The second battalion of The Fourth sent
out cards for a ball, last winter, and a round
dozen of them turned up in our mail at headquarters. As a rule, we never allow an in-
vitation from that part of the world to go
unheeded; but this time we had to return
our really regretful regrets, because a meeting of the council of officers had been ordered
for that particular night. It was too bad.

But The Third, if for nothing more than

old acquaintance' sake, had to be represented. And so the colonel, after thoughtfully considering the varied attractions of the staff, sent for the quartermaster — " Woodleigh, Q.M.," he signs himself, when the paper is an official one — and, after loading him down with his blessing and our compliments to the fellows of the other corps, regretfully saw him start off alone towards the scene of impending festivities. " Woodleigh's a fine shape of man," the colonel argued to himself, " and he'll do for a sample of the rest of us. Besides, what earthly sort of use *are* quartermasters, except for ornament? " So off went Woodleigh to the ball.

In course of time he came back again, telling strange things about what had happened to him during his absence.

" About that ball? " said he, on a night in the following week, when a half-dozen of us had bunched ourselves before one of old Sam's master-pieces of fire-building, up in The Battery. " Oh, well, it was a big ball, a broad-and-wide ball, a very large ball indeed. You missed it by not going. The armory was decorated right up to the vanishing-point — out of sight, in fact. There were brass

twelve-pounders on each side of the Gover-
nor's box, like signs to call attention to the
big guns inside of it; and there were oceans
of bunting; and all the regimental colors
that The Fourth has had issued to it in the
last thirty years; and jungles of palms and
other green things; and girls — yes, there
were girls, of course.

"There was *one* girl — Never mind: that
wouldn't interest you fellows.   But perhaps
you'd like to hear about the supper.   There
was a very nourishing supper, so they tell
me.   I didn't stay for it, though."

With our knowledge of the quartermaster's
customary prowess at the banquet table, this
last statement seemed to call for farther explanation.   We ventured to ask him about it.

"Why did I cut that supper?   Well, because I wanted to.   Why did I want to?
H'm! you're hot for information, aren't you?
But perhaps I may as well tell you.   If I
don't, somebody else will; and if it has to be
told, I'd prefer to have it told truthfully.

"It was all on account of that girl — that
one girl.   I'm not ashamed to admit that it
was a case of utter annihilation at first sight.
I had hardly stepped out upon the armory

floor, when my eye fell on her ; and from that
instant I knew that, for *me*, there wasn't
another girl in that whole hall — no, nor in
the whole wide world. 'See anybody you'd
like to meet ?' says Major Brayton, who
had me under his wing. 'Yes, present me
to that stunning girl in yellow,' says I, like
a flash ; 'that girl sitting over there beside
the stout woman in black.' Confound Brayton ! he might have warned me. But he
didn't : he only grinned and said 'Perhaps
you'd better get Erwin to take you up. But
come along with me, I'll risk it.'

"Whew ! she *was* a tearing beauty. Big,
soft, brown eyes, and a regular cloud of
wavy, brown hair to match, and a general
effect of having just stepped out of one of
Gibson's drawings. When the major presented me, my heart was thumping like a
bass-drum. Fact ! Her name ? I didn't
quite catch it. But I captured her card, and
signed contracts for a waltz, and some sort
of country-dance just after it, and another
waltz well along towards the end of the list.
How did I score her down on *my* card?
Why, I just scratched down 'D' — which
might have stood for most anything.

" Well, we floated through the waltz. It was a treat, for she was a divine dancer, as I'd thought she'd be. When the country-dance came along, I suggested that we'd do well to hunt up some place in the gallery from which we could look down upon it, explaining that I was a little weak in my minor tactics, and really didn't feel up to getting tangled in any such complicated manœuvres unless I had a book of directions with me. So up to the gallery we went, and I found an ideal corner, all hidden by bunting draperies, and palms and things.

"And there we sat — just we two — in a ready-made paradise of our own, utterly forgetful of the crush of prancing idiots who were toiling away on the floor below us. H'm! I think I must have lost my head completely. I said all sorts of things. As a matter of fact, I can't begin to remember half what I *did* say. I only know that finally the music stopped, and she rose with a sigh. ' Can't I steal this next dance?' says I, taking her card from her to see who the lucky man was that had it. ' No,' says she softly, ' I'm afraid that it wouldn't be possible.' I glanced at the card, and for the first time

noticed that the next dance and fully two-
thirds of the others were labelled '*J. E.*', in a
painfully distinct and careful hand.

"And while I was assimilating this interesting fact, who should come blundering into
our little, private paradise but Jack Erwin,
first lieutenant of 'C', Fourth. You don't
know him? Wish *I* didn't! 'Hello! Woodleigh, old man,' says he, grabbing my paw.
'Found you at last. They told me you were
doing guard duty for me. Well, I'm waiting to be congratulated.'

"'I beg pardon, Jack,' says I; 'promotion?' And then he laughed — one of those
silly, cheerful, lover's laughs — and tucked
my girl's slender little hand under his arm.
'No,' says he; 'or, rather, yes. Hadn't you
heard of my engagement?' And he smiled
down on the girl in a way that made me wild
to toss him over the balcony railing.

"But I didn't. I simply pulled myself together as best I could, and shook hands with
him, and mumbled something or other to her,
and then watched them go strolling off together. And just as they went out of sight
behind the palms, I saw her press closer to

him, and heard her say, ' Oh, Jack, dear, I thought you never *would* come ! '

"That's all I know about the ball. If you're still thirsting for points on it, I'll refer you to Whateley, of ' H ' troop. He was there. Danced all night, I believe, and generally did his duty. Queer boy, Whateley! It made me sorrowful to see him wasting his time in that way, when he might have been putting it in to better advantage. But then, the ' Yellow-Legs ' are always great on dismounted duty ; nothing short of ' Boots-and-Saddles ' ever rattles a really and truly volunteer trooper."

Little Poore had wandered over to the bookcase, and was standing before it, thumbing over the pages of the latest adjutant-general's report. " The first lieutenant of ' *C* ', *Fourth*, is here put down as one Wilkins," he said, turning towards us. " I don't seem to find the name of Erwin anywhere in the register."

Woodleigh calmly looked over at him, and then addressed the rest of us. " You'll have to excuse him. He hasn't been with us long, and doesn't quite understand my ways," he explained. " Very likely he thought I'd have the bad taste to lug real names into a personal story of that sort. Come back here, Poore, and sit down. You must learn to save yourself all un-necessary trouble." Poore put away his book, and returned to his place in the family circle.

"Care to hear anything more about my adventures, up there with The Fourth?" inquired Woodleigh, rising and taking up a more congenial position, with his back to the crackling fire. "Because, if you do, there was another odd thing that happened that evening. After my heart had been broken, in the way that I've told you, Tileson, the Q.M. of The Fourth, ran up against me. He noticed that I wasn't quite in gear. 'You're looking faint,' says he. 'Come along with me, and I'll see if something can't be done for you. This ball business is all childish folly.' Tileson, you know, isn't a dancing man.

"Well, he took me away from the armory, and over to the club — you fellows remember that club they have up there? — and we played billiards and other games for a while. Tileson also fixed me up with restoratives until I felt quite like myself again; for he ranks high as a scientific quartermaster.

Finally we sat down to smoke, and while we were smoking we got to talking shop.

"I don't remember just what led up to it, but we drifted along from one thing to another until we got into a discussion on athletics. Well, you know how it goes: Tileson began to yarn about what he used to do in that line, when he was younger; and that, of course, started me into recalling certain feats of my own long-gone youth; and so we had it, back and forth, until Tileson ended up by wanting to make some fool-bet or other. And right at that point I conceived an idea.

"You see, it was growing late, and I found that I was becoming sleepier than a stewed owl. Besides, that club was full of men, and thick with smoke; and I wanted to get away from the confounded noise and chatter. I'd engaged a room at the hotel, and had left my bag there; for I'd made my plans to stay in town all night — but, as I said, I was attacked by an idea.

"'Tileson,' says I, after the idea in all its beauty had paraded itself before my mind's eye, 'I'm not a betting man. And least of all will I bet money. Playing for money invariably leads to hard feelings. His Imperial

Majesty, the Emperor of Germany, and likewise I, Woodleigh, Q.M. of The Third, frown
down upon all gambling among officers, both
of us holding that it is detrimental to the best
interests of the service. But I'll tell you
what I'll do for your amusement: I'll make
you a wager of a small dinner. *That's* not
gambling, because we both have to eat
dinner, every day in the week, for which
somebody has to pay. Am I correct?'

"Tileson had to admit that a daily dinner
was of the nature of a necessity, and that it
wouldn't be gambling to risk one. So I proceeded to spread out the details of my proposition. 'It is a bright, moon-lighted night,'
says I, after taking a peek at my watch for
certain reasons of my own; 'there's no snow
on the ground, and there's not a breath of
wind: therefore a paper trail would lie beautifully — which is something that I person-
ally can't do. Why wouldn't it be an educated scheme to arrange a hare-and-hounds
chase, as a means of settling this speed question?'

"This seemed to strike Tileson as a grand
thought, and so I went right along with my
remarks. 'Of course,' says I, 'I'll be handi-

capped by not knowing the country, but I'm reasonably certain that I can start out from this club with two minutes lee-way, and lead you a chase for forty-five minutes, without being caught. I'll carry a basketful of paper, and drop a handful of it, every twenty yards, as long as it lasts. I'll also agree not to enter any house or building during that three-quarters of an hour; my time shall be entirely devoted to going cross-country. Moreover, after leaving the club, and making one turn, I'll lay my course in a crow-line — I mean, as the bee flies — for a distance of at least a half-mile, thereby giving you a chance to run me down by a straight-away sprint. Now, what do you say?'

"'It's a go!' says Tileson, gobbling down the bait, without a thought for any hook that might be hidden inside it. 'Well,' says I; 'that's all I wanted to know. Now I'll just slide over to the hotel, and shift out of these togs. I'm not going to travel cross-country in a brand-new dress uniform. Can't afford it. I shall have to insist on entering for the event in citizen's dress. I'll be back in a minute, and we'll draw up final articles.'

" Naturally, Tileson claimed the same privilege, and made a break for home, to change his outfit; while I tooled across to the hotel, to look after a few arrangements of my own. First, I rushed up to my room, stripped off my full-dress, and packed it into my travelling bag, strapping my overcoat on the outside, with my sword snugly tucked underneath it. Then I went down to the office, explained that I had made other plans for the night, paid my bill, and asked for the night porter. I bought him outright with a shining half-dollar, took him into a corner, and carefully coached him in the part I'd laid out for him to play in my programme. Furthermore, I grabbed a sheet of paper, and wrote out exactly what I wished him to do, so that there could be no possible slip-up. And then, having given him my bag and his written orders, I went back to the club.

"I got there just before Tileson. When he came in, the fellows sent up a yell that opened great cracks in the plastering, for he appeared in the most marvellous get-up that ever was seen outside of comic opera. I hadn't believed it, but it seems that, in his day, he really used to be something of an amateur athlete. Well, he'd gone down into

his old-clothes box, and had fished out all
the sporty duds that he could lay hand to :
and there he stood, after he'd thrown off his
ulster, in a pair of spiked running shoes, his
legs bare to the knee, a pair of white flannel
knickerbockers coming next, a striped sweater
a-top of that, and a faded old rowing cap
crowning the whole crazy-quilt combination.
It was very obvious that he hadn't appeared
in his nondescript regalia for some time pre-
viously, for the billiard room reeked like an
apothecary shop with the odor of camphor.

" Wasn't he a gaudy object ! I had to sit
down to laugh, and it really was quite a time
before I got into shape enough to put in a
protest against his turning up in such light
marching order as that. But it was no use.
He maintained that his rig was citizen's dress
and nothing else, and the rest of the fellows
backed him up in his claim. So I gracefully
yielded the point. 'If this isn't citizen's
dress, what *is* it ? ' says he. He certainly had
me there.

" By this time the excitement in that club
was quoted at a high figure. It was after
two o'clock in the morning, and the men
were beginning to drop in from the ball in

squads. At least a dozen of The Fourth's officers were there, besides a lot from out of town. All the odds were on Tileson — nobody had the nerve to bet against that fearful and wonderful rig of his.

"Well, we sent a select committee into the reading-room, and set them at work tearing up the old papers on the files for the 'scent' that was to be left along my trail. And they worked with a will, until they'd filled a waste-basket heaping full. Then we selected judges, and umpires, and referees, and time-keepers, until about everybody in the place had some office or other. And all the while I kept one eye on the clock that stood in the corner of the billiard-room. It was an old-fashioned, tall clock, and I'd noted the fact that it was eleven minutes slow. This, I'll state, made it necessary for me to perform some wonderful problems in mental arithmetic; and trying to figure, in the midst of the row that was going on up there, wasn't any intellectual picnic. I managed it, though.

"Now, the billiard-room was at the rear, and in the third story, of the club-house, and we'd agreed that the start should be made from it. This, of course, was because I didn't care to have anybody know just what I was up to during the first two minutes of the race. I also had stipulated that Tileson and all hands should stay in that room until my time-limit had expired. Well, when the venerable clock alleged that it was two-thirty-nine, I tucked the waste-paper basket under my arm, shook hands with Tileson, and got on my marks at the head of the stairway. 'Start me at two-forty,' says I, scooping up a fistful of paper, and nodding up towards the clock. ''*Tention!*' sang out Major Brayton, whom we'd made head time-keeper. 'By the numbers: one — two — *go!*' And at that I pitched a bunch of torn paper up into the air, so that Tileson wouldn't have any trouble in finding where my trail began, and then bundled myself down those stairs like a thousand of brick.

"But as soon as I landed on the sidewalk, I took it more easily; for two minutes' start was ample for my requirements. I lighted a cigar, and then headed down the street at an ordinary gait, conscientiously dropping paper at every twenty yards. You may bet that I didn't run: I wasn't planning to have any country policeman scoop *me* in for a suspicious character. Wherein I displayed great brain-power.

"Now, the club up there, you'll remember, is located on the main street of the town. Very likely you'll remember also that the railway station lies only about a hundred yards down the street from the club-house. Furthermore, the tracks of the railway run across that street at grade, in the comfortably reckless way that they have in towns of that size. Well, now you have the whole situation, and you can see, of course, what my plan of campaign was like.

"I'd recalled the fact, while I was talking with Tileson, that the down mail-train from Canada was due to strike the town at two-forty-eight, and was scheduled to continue its run to the eastward at two-fifty-three. I happened to know, too, that it seldom picked up any passengers at that hour of the night : that, in fact, it stopped mainly for the purpose of watering the engine and juggling mail-bags. So I felt fairly confident that nobody would suspect me of having any designs on *that* particular method of performing a cross-country run. And events proved that I was right.

" Well, after I'd cleared the club, I strolled down the street and took up my position alongside the track, just as the locomotive gave a warning snort and came slowly pulling out from the station. I looked at my watch. It showed two-fifty-three, to a second. I turned and glanced towards the club, and saw a white figure come shooting out into the moonlight, followed by a running accompaniment of darker shapes. And then, as the engine went puffing past, I faced towards the train.

"It gathered headway slowly, and the first cars seemed to crawl by me. But by the time the baggage-car, mail-car, and a pair of ordinary coaches had gone lumbering past, the whole outfit was making pretty fair speed ; and when I grabbed the handrail of the Pullman which came along as rear guard to the whole procession, I had to hop like a monkey with Saint Vitus' dance. I got aboard all right, though, and brought my paper-basket with me, without spilling more than a reasonable amount of its contents. And then I looked back, and saw things happening.

" Now, while I was standing by the track,

waiting for the Pullman to get within board-
ing distance, I'd heard, above the roar of the
train, a perfect pandemonium of other sounds.
But I hadn't had the nerve to look behind
me, because I knew that I'd have to make
pretty close connections with my handrail,
when it came along.   I was painfully aware
that I should have a narrow squeak in getting away; for the distance from the club was
so short that Tileson stood a very brilliant
show of covering it before the train could
gather headway enough to save me from
being run down.   And, if it hadn't been for
a providential miracle, I'm inclined to think
that I should have had to pay for that dinner,
after all.   But the miracle got there just in
the nick of time.

"It seems that it's the custom of the one
policeman on night duty in that town to go
to the station to meet all trains, whereby he
keeps himself awake and exercises a sort of
general supervision over the in-comings and
out-goings of the populace.   Well, as the
train left the station, the policeman saun-
tered out upon the main street, just in time
to see coming tearing towards him a wild man
in indecent garments, followed by a mob of

panting pursuers. Naturally enough he saw before him the chance of a lifetime; and so he pulled himself into shape, tackled Tileson, and down they went in a wild snarl of arms and legs and bad language. And that's what I saw as I stood there on the rear platform; for it was a bright, moonlight night, and everything was as plain as print. The show didn't last long for me, though, because the train was humming along on a straight stretch of track, and in a little while the smoke and dust streamed out in its wake, like a curtain falling on the last act of a tragedy. Did I laugh? *Did* I? I did — until I came perilously near rolling off the car! I kept my wits about me, though, and religiously dealt out torn paper, every twenty yards, until it was all gone. I didn't forget that I'd made a solemn agreement to leave behind me a plain and continuous trail.

"At the rate at which we were spinning along it didn't take a great while to exhaust my supply of 'scent.' When the last of it was gone, I kicked the basket overboard, and went inside the car. And there I found my luggage waiting me, and a berth all engaged;

for my man from the hotel had followed his orders to the letter.

"Now, I'd like to ask you if that wasn't quite an event in amateur athletics? I hold that the cross-country championship belongs to The Third; and I also claim that I scored on Tileson and his suit of many colors." On which points the sentiment of the meeting seemed to be with Woodleigh.

A day or two afterwards one of us happened to run across Whateley. "That man Woodleigh, of yours, is a corker!" said he. "After I left the ball, the other night, I went up to that club where The Fourth's fellows hang out. Got there just after Woodleigh had gone sailing off in a chariot of fire, like old what's-his-name. Well, it was worth a four-cornered gold brick to hear 'em rubbing it into Tileson! Did you know he came within an inch of being pulled in for assaulting a constable? Oh, he'll never hear the last of it! I'd like to go you five that he sends in his papers before next camp. Old Woodleigh didn't cut a very wide swath at the dance, though. Did he tell you about it? He was paired off with a little, stumpy, freckle-faced girl, and had to tramp nine laps 'round the hall with her in the 'Grand March,' so called. Perhaps he wasn't the picture of misery! He and Tileson escaped, right after the march; sneaked for the club before the music struck up for the first waltz. Really, you fellows ought to send somebody else besides Woodleigh to represent you on occasions of that sort. He doesn't do his duty."

THE KERWICK CUP.

THE KERWICK CUP.

ELSEWHERE in the annals of The Third it has been stated — and the statement proven — that Major Pollard can shoot. Here it will be shown that he can shoot not only well, but also most thoughtfully.

It was the night before Christmas. Pollard was walking slowly along the street, on his way home from the theater. He felt at peace with himself and with all the rest of the world; for that afternoon, by a despairing and truly heroic effort, he had managed to dispatch a half-dozen neat parcels conveying to the immediate members of his family the greetings appropriate to the season. And this was an achievement of no small magnitude; for everybody knows how difficult it is to pick out various sorts of gifts for various sorts of people, especially when certain of

those people are women, and the giver of the
gifts has the misfortune to be a man — and
a single one.   Which will explain, it may
be, why so many men get themselves married, and then straightway delegate to their
wives full authority in the matter of select-
ing presents.

The air was keen.   A light, powdery snow
came lazily drifting down, only to find its
whiteness quickly lost upon the much trav-
eled pavement.   A red-cheeked newsboy,
whining the old, old story about being
"stuck," placed himself in Pollard's path;
and the major, in the true spirit of Christmas-
tide, was exploring his pocket in search of
the necessary bit of silver — when, full in the
glare of an electric lamp, there came into
sight a figure that somehow seemed familiar.

Stopping short in his hunt for a dime, Pollard stared hard at the approaching form; and
then, tossing to the expectant urchin the first
coin upon which his fingers chanced to close,
he started in pursuit of his man, who already
had passed him, and was going at a rate of
speed that made it probable that in another
minute he would be lost to view in the midst
of the theater crowd upon the sidewalk.

A few rapid strides brought the major to his side, and a last, quick glance satisfied him that he had not been mistaken. "Hello, Kerwick," said he, laying his hand upon the shoulder of the other. "Thought I couldn't be wrong. Well, well! I'm more than glad to see you back again."

At the sound of Pollard's voice the man stopped and shrank away. He had been walking rapidly along, with head lowered and eyes fixed upon the ground, as if to avoid any chance recognition. He wore no overcoat, and the collar of his shiny, black cutaway was turned up to protect his throat from the biting night air. Taken as a whole, he was not a cheerful object to contemplate.

"Ah, it's you, Pollard, is it?" he said, with a side glance at the major. "How are you? I'm just back from the West today. Nasty night, isn't it?"

"Yes," assented Pollard, noting that his ill-conditioned friend could with difficulty keep from shivering; "too nasty for making visits on the curbstone. I'm just going to raid some place for oysters and other hot things. You'll join me, Captain?"

At the sound of this title the other drew

himself up a bit; but in an instant he fell back a pace, flushing painfully. "Join you?" he said bitterly, thrusting his be-numbed hands deeply into his trousers' pock-ets; "join *you!* Good God, Pollard, look at me!"

"Well, I *am* looking at you," said the major, allowing his gaze to travel slowly up and down the shrinking figure before him. "You certainly look terribly seedy, and not much like the Captain Kerwick under whom I used to serve. But if that's any reason for your refusing to sit down to half-a-dozen Blue-Points with me, why, I simply fail to see it."

"I'll not do it," said the other doggedly. "No, Pollard, I'll not do it. I'm out of your world, and you're out of mine. That's the long and short of it. Possibly you no-ticed that I didn't say I was glad to see you? Well, I'm not. I'm confoundedly sorry I set eyes on you; or, rather, that you set eyes on me. Will you let me go *now?* Good night."

Without a word in reply to this outbreak, Pollard slipped an arm under that of his friend, and used the other to aid his voice in

attracting the attention of a passing cab.
When the vehicle pulled up beside the curb-
ing, he wrenched open the door, good-nat-
uredly pushed in his prisoner, and followed,
after having given to the driver the address
of his cosey bachelor rooms in an up-town
hotel.

"My dear man," said he, drawing up the
heavy robe and carefully tucking it around
his thinly clad companion, "it's useless for
you to protest. There's been a change since
you were lord high autocrat of 'M' Company.
I've climbed up from lieutenant to captain,
and then from captain to major; so you
can see the utter folly of trying to dispute
my commands. You'll have to submit, Kerwick, and you'll do well to submit gracefully."

"And now," said Pollard, twenty minutes
later, after he had settled his captive in a big
arm-chair before the glowing coal fire in his
rooms, "now we'll consider the question of
supper, first. Other matters may wait their
turn. You may bring up," to the neatly
uniformed colored boy who had appeared in
answer to his vigorous assault upon the electric bell, "two half-dozens of oysters on the

shell, and a small tenderloin steak, fairly well-done, and a bottle of — " He gave a side glance at the man seated before his fire. " And a pot of coffee," he amended.

" That last was well thought of," said Kerwick, as the bell boy left the room. " You're still observant, I see. Well, you've guessed it ; the bottle has held altogether too prominent a place in my recent history."

The ruins of the supper had been cleared away. Kerwick was again installed before the fire, with a cigar. Pollard lighted his old black briar, pulled a chair towards the hearth, and said, as he seated himself, " We're not to have a green Yuletide, this year, after all. It's snowing in earnest now."

" H'm ! tomorrow's Christmas," murmured Kerwick, with something like a sigh. " So it is. I hadn't thought much about it. Well, Pollard, you haven't asked me yet — but I suppose you're waiting for me to give an account of myself."

The major nodded, and smoked on in silence while his friend told the story of the past few years: How he had broken away from all his early associations in order to grasp at what had seemed a chance for making rapid fortune in the West; how reverses had come quickly, one upon another, until — baffled and beaten at every point — he had yielded under the repeated blows, and finally had staggered and gone down beneath the weight of discouragement.

"And here I am, back again," Kerwick wound up, flinging into the fire his half finished cigar, as if its flavor brought to him some of the bitterness of recent disappointment; "here I am, at forty-five, in what should be the prime of my life — homeless, hopeless, penniless, and out of the game."

"Yes?" said Pollard, as the other finished. "Now, old man, see here: you're not to throw away my cigars in the same careless way in which you've thrown away your chances. They're too choice, if I do say it, to be handled disrespectfully. Take another, and *smoke* it." He pushed the box across the table towards Kerwick. "These weeds were made to be burned — but not in open grates."

Kerwick laughed shortly, picked a fresh cigar from the box, and lighted it. "You'll have to pardon me," said he. "That was temporary insanity. I haven't smoked a decent cigar, before these, in nobody knows how many months."

"Now, as for your croaking," resumed Pollard, giving emphasis to his remarks by an occasional thump of his heavy fist upon the arm of his chair; "I'm going to make the only comment that seems to fit the case. Which is, '*Stuff!*' For you're playing now with nothing to lose and everything to win. Why, Kerwick, you *must* see it! Nothing from nothing leaves nothing; but nothing plus something may amount to almost anything. Confound you, old man! I used to look up to you as the embodiment of grit and push — and I'll not let you tumble down in my estimation, nor in your own."

"Too late, Polly," answered Kerwick in a low tone, half unconsciously letting fall a nickname of the old days. "You mean well, but it's too late — it's too late now."

"Blessed if it isn't!" exclaimed the major, putting upon the words of the other a construction of his own. "It's quarter to twelve, and high old time for us to be sliding into bed. There's a good day's work cut out for both of us tomorrow. I dare say you haven't forgotten the bit of silverware that used to go by the name of 'The Kerwick Cup'? Well, tomorrow we shoot for it."

Now, it might be well to mention that Kerwick, in the prosperous days when he was captain of "M" Company, was a rifleman of great enthusiasm, and of no small skill. And when, on leaving for the West, he resigned his commission, he gave to his old command, as memorials of his interest in the most manly of all sports, two trophies — The Kerwick Cup, and The Kerwick Medal. These were to be shot for in annual competition : the medal, by the enlisted men ; the cup, by the active and past officers of the company. And for a number of years it had been the custom to shoot both these matches on the forenoon of Christmas day.

"Are those old things still in existence?" asked the captain, with a slight show of interest. "Really! I'd half forgotten them. But then," wearily, "I've forgotten most of the things in which I ever found any pleasure."

"Bah! you couldn't forget the fun we've had together ; no, not for the life of you," Pollard burst out impatiently. "Well, the old cup's still waiting to be won ; and so's the medal. Sergeant Harvey — he was a corporal in your day, wasn't he? — won the medal three times straight, which nearly gave it to him for keeps. But he's out of the service now. The cup? Oh, I'm bidding high myself for the cup. My name's been engraved on it for three years, hand-running, and tomorrow may or may not send it my way for the fourth and final holding."

"Ah, yes, I remember now," said Kerwick; "both the old things had to be won four times consecutively in order to pass the title. I hope you'll pull out all right, Pollard; I'd be glad to know that the mug was decorating your mantel. I'll look for your score in the papers. Well, as you say, it's growing late. You've given me a very pleasant evening, and I'd like to tell you how it has brought back old times, being up here with you in this way — but perhaps I needn't. Good night." And with this he rose, buttoned his thin black coat closely about him, and held out his hand.

In an instant Pollard was upon his feet. "What the deuce are you thinking of doing?" he demanded, placing himself by a sudden movement between Kerwick and the door. "Going to leave me, eh? Not much! You're my prisoner, sir; sit down."

For a minute the captain faced Pollard, with an appealing look upon his face; but he ended by yielding to the stronger will, and obediently dropped back into his chair. The major came over to the fireplace, and took up his position upon the hearthrug, with his back to the fire. His teeth were firmly set upon the amber mouthpiece of his pipe, and as he spoke he punctuated his sentences with an occasional short puff of smoke. " Now pay attention to what I'm saying to you," he began, looking down kindly upon the man before him, " because it has ' Official ' stamped all over it, and it's not to be disputed about, nor argued over."

" Six years ago," said Pollard, letting himself drop back until his broad shoulders rested comfortably against the high mantel-shelf, " you and I were good friends. As I recall it, we used to find life rather a pleasant sort of thing. But, not content with leaving well enough alone, you had to send yourself chasing away after the pot of gold at the foot of the western rainbow. Well, luck didn't run your way: either you didn't hold openers, or else the pot was buried too deeply to be easily got at — and here you are, back again, after having made a most praiseworthy attempt at going to the devil."

" Is this a sermon ? " asked Kerwick, at this point in Pollard's discourse.

" No, it isn't," said the major earnestly; " at least, it's not meant for one. But what I'm getting at is this : you've got to borrow a leaf from the politician's book, and 'put yourself into the hands of your friends.' Now, we can't map out a whole career for you at a single sitting ; so we'll simply settle the programme for the next forty-eight hours, and call it a night's work at that."

" Thanks ! " said Kerwick dryly. " To tell the truth, I *don't* feel quite up to arranging my future at the present moment."

" No ? " said Pollard. " Neither do I. But you may consider this much of it as having been already arranged: tomorrow we go out with the company, shoot in the cup match — you may win your own mug, if you're lucky enough — then we come back to town, dine together, and wind up the day with an old-fashioned evening of yarning and smoking, up here in these rooms ; day after tomorrow, we consider what's to be done with you ; after that, we begin to do it. See?"

"I wish I could, Polly," began Kerwick, "but —"

"Oh, about clothes and things," broke in the major; "I can fit you out to a button. We go out in fatigue, you know, tomorrow: well, when I got my last promotion, I was so tickled over it that I treated myself to a whole new outfit, so I've my captain's uniform still on hand, and it'll fit you like wall paper unless you've changed several sizes since last we ran together."

The clock upon the mantel began to strike. From without, hushed and mellowed by the thickly falling snow, came the sound of the chimes in old St. Luke's.

"Hello! it's morning," said Pollard, as the clock's deep-toned gong told off the last stroke of midnight. "Merry Christmas, Kerwick! *Merry Christmas, old man!* Got ahead of you that time, didn't I? And now we must crawl under the blankets, for in ten hours from now we'll be bullseye chasing."

Kerwick slowly rose from his chair. He placed both hands on Pollard's shoulders, looked him full in the face, and said, "God bless you, Polly!" And then, the least bit huskily, he added, "Perhaps you're right, after all. Perhaps it s *not* too late."

Pollard saw his old commander safely stowed away in the little box of a room that he was pleased to call his guest chamber, and then went about his preparations for the coming match. First, he put in order his rifle, and filled his thimble belt with half a hundred cartridges of his own careful loading. Then, after laying out his own uniform, he hunted through closet and wardrobe until he had got together a captain's full outfit, which he placed upon a chair, just outside the door of Kerwick's room.

For a moment he stood there listening. From within came the sound of deep, regular breathing. He softly turned the knob, and stepped into the room. Kerwick lay sound asleep, with his face turned towards the wall. Feeling like a full-fledged thief, Pollard laid hands upon the waistcoat which hung at the head of the bed, and then stealthily crept out of the room.

There was no watch in the waistcoat. Pollard opened a drawer of his desk, took out a plain silver timepiece — a relic of his school days — wound and set it, and slipped it into its proper pocket. He explored the other pockets. In one he found a ragged two dollar bill; in another, a stub of pencil and a card of common matches. That was all.

Tossing the vulgar brimstone matches into the fire, he went again to his desk and rummaged about until he found a silver match box — one of many that had come to him on birthdays and other times of the sort — which he filled with parlor matches and placed in the lower, left-hand pocket. Then he drew out a roll of bills, picked out three crisp fives, folded them up, once lengthwise and once across, with Kerwick's poor, tattered banknote, and tucked the money snugly into the lower, right-hand pocket. And then he stole back into the captain's room, and hung the garment in the place in which he had found it.

" Poor devil! He's utterly done up," he said to himself, as he left the room, after a last glance at his sleeping guest. " And no wonder! Well, there's another Santa Claus tradition gone wrong! I haven't put anything into the old chap's socks. Never mind. The chances are that they're too full of holes to make the filling of 'em a possibility."

He went over to the mantel, filled a leather cigar case with *Perfectos*, and stowed it away in the inner pocket of the fatigue jacket which lay ready for Kerwick to don in the morning. This done, he stood thinking for a moment before the fire, and then, beginning rapidly to throw off his clothes, he muttered, "Yes, that will work. It's *sure* to!" With which truly oracular remark he started off to bed.

Christmas day came in under a clear sky. Pollard rose at an early hour, went to the window for a hasty glance at the snowy world outside, and then rapped noisily at his friend's door, singing out cheerily, "Hi! Kerwick. Time you were getting up." And to hasten matters, he whistled the bars of *Reveille*, the lively call which, many a time, had brought them tumbling out from their blankets when under canvas with the Old Regiment.

Kerwick's night of untroubled sleep had worked wonders. After a dip into the bath, and ten minutes' careful work with the razor, he looked another man. And when at last, arrayed in captain's uniform, he had inspected himself in Pollard's mirror, he faced about, threw back his shoulders, and said with a healthy ring in his voice, " Polly, my

son, I've been pretty far down, but I'll live up
to my old rank again — if only for today."

"Did anybody ever see such a fit?" asked
Pollard, gazing admiringly at the natty appearance of his friend. "Talk about being
melted and poured into clothes! Why, that
blouse looks as if it had been frescoed on
you."

Kerwick passed his hand over the breast of
the snugly clinging blouse, and became
aware, in doing it, that something lay hidden
beneath its surface. Unbuttoning it, he drew
out the cigar case. "Ah, that was thoughtful of you," said he. "Thank you, Polly."

Struck by a sudden thought, he ran his
fingers into the pocket where the lone bill
had been. The modest wad of money came
into view. He colored slightly, and then
tried a second pocket, whereby he discovered
the little silver watch, which looked him
boldly in the face, and promptly ticked out
its holiday greeting. In its turn, too, the
match box came to light. And all the while
Pollard stood by, surveying the proceedings
with a grin of satisfied approval.

"The match box and the matches in it,"
explained the major, "are from Santa Claus.

The same applies to the cigar case and its contents. The watch and those few bills are a loan from me; you'll return 'em when it's most convenient. And now we must be moving."

The two ex-captains breakfasted together, and then hastened down to the station for the early morning train. With a little group of other past officers they were standing upon the platform, when the shrill squeak of a fife and the lively rattle of a drum came clearly on the crisp December air, to warn them that the boys were drawing near. And in a moment, to the tune of *The Bold MacIntyre*, the company came swinging in through the wide doorway and down the long platform, making the vaulted roof of the trainhouse resound with the steady tramp, tramp, tramp of the marching column.

Three officers, white-gloved and trim; fifty men, muffled in the blue great-coats of the service; fifty rifles sloping at the trail; belts black and glossy, buttons and brasses glittering like polished mirrors — it all went to make as bright a picture of the pomp and circumstance of volunteering as one could wish to see.

The train slowly pulled out from the long station, bearing the jolly little army towards its peaceful battle ground. Pollard settled Kerwick safely at the forward end of the car, with Colonel Elliott, and then industriously began the final development of the grand idea which had taken shape in his brain the night before. One after another he button-holed the dozen or so officers in the car, attacking each one somewhat after this fashion:

" Here's old Kerwick back again. Seems good to see him, doesn't it? Blamed good fellow, if ever there was one! Well, he's been having a horrible run of luck lately. I happen to know that he's hard pushed, and is worrying over it. But he's clear sand, grit 'way through to the vertebræ — and none of us ever will find out from *him* how he's been getting it in the neck. Now, I want to fix up a sort of benefit for him. You'll help me out in it? Of course; knew you would. But we can't chip in to *give* him anything. He's too infernally proud: wouldn't have it, you know.

" Here's what I'd propose: we'll make up a sweepstake in the cup match, throw in five dollars apiece, and then let Kerwick win the whole business. None of us will be killed by dropping a fiver, but the aggregate pot will give the old chap quite a lift. He used to shoot like a demon once. Don't know if he can now — but we can make sure that we shoot worse than he does, anyway. We'll have to do all this quietly, on account of the men; 'twouldn't do to have 'em get the idea that we're gambling. Grand strategy on a small scale, isn't it?" And with this, Pollard would release that particular victim, and start off in search of yet another recruit for his enterprise.

The annual shoot of "M" Company certainly was a notable success. The Kerwick Medal was won on the phenomenal score of thirty-three points, in seven shots; and no less than sixteen of the fifty men competing for it managed to roll up an average of centers, or better. But when it came to the struggle for the Kerwick *Cup* — well, that was a different matter!

Pollard quietly had collected the entries for the sweepstake, and had turned over the money to Colonel Elliott, who — not being a past officer of the company — could not shoot for the cup. He had some difficulty in getting Kerwick into the match, but finally succeeded in persuading him that it would look odd if he, with his past reputation as a rifle sharp, should persist in staying out. There were twelve competitors in all, and consequently the colonel found himself the custodian of sixty dollars' worth of the Government's paper.

The match began. Colonel Hamilton, of the retired list, and Captain Bromstead, of the active company, made the first pair. Bromstead has rather educated ideas about the handling of a rifle, and Colonel Hamilton seldom scatters much lead outside the four ring; but in this particular match the shooting of both was something fearful to behold and wonderful to reflect upon. For the captain's seven shots netted just twenty-one points, while Hamilton, after piling up an even twenty, fell back from the firing point in well feigned disgust.

And so it went, as pair after pair took their turn at the targets, until — amid a storm of good-natured chaffing — all except Kerwick and Pollard had fired. Up to this point, the top score was twenty-five. It had been made by little Poore, junior lieutenant of the company, who afterwards apologized to Pollard for doing such brilliant work, explaining that, by way of experiment, he had closed both eyes when firing his last shot, by which means — to his utter astonishment and no small chagrin — he had plumped his bullet dead into the center of the bullseye.

"Major Pollard and Captain Kerwick!" called the scorer. Kerwick stepped quickly to his place, and the major slowly followed.

"After you, Pollard," said Kerwick, with a nod towards the targets, to signify that the major should lead off.

"No, no, Captain," said Pollard; "after you. I'm defending the cup, you know, and it's my privilege to see what I must shoot against."

Kerwick tested the pull of his piece, looked keenly at the sights, gave just the slightest touch to the wind-gauge, slipped in a cartridge, and then leveled the long barrel upon the target. For three seconds he stood motionless, and then he fired. It was a bullseye. The group behind him sent up a murmur of applause, which was promptly checked by Colonel Elliott. Pollard threw his piece easily to his shoulder, aimed quickly, fired, and brought up a bullseye in his turn.

Kerwick's second shot was a close four; Pollard's, another bullseye. On the third attempt, Kerwick again found the black, while the major's shot was a very chilly center. After the sixth round had been completed, the captain stepped back and glanced at the scorer's blackboard. The story then read :

Captain Kerwick 5, 4, 5, 4, 4, 5
Major Pollard 5, 5, 4, 4, 4, 5

He went back to his place, and passed his hand across his eyes, as if to drive away the dazzling glare of the sun upon the snow. Barring a bright red spot on either cheek, his face was ashen pale. Those who were watching him closely noticed that his knees were slightly trembling.

Among the officers in rear of the firing point there was suppressed excitement. Little Poore drew Bromstead aside, and in a whisper confided to him his opinion that Pollard was a combination of pirate, bunco-steerer, and all-'round brute. He also hinted at the advisability of jamming a handful of snow down the back of Pollard's neck, in order to disarrange his nervous system. Colonel Elliott, with one hand deep in his trousers' pocket, savagely clutching the roll of bills confided to his keeping, stood blackly scowling at Pollard, and endeavoring to catch his eye. But the major calmly went on with the operation of blowing through the barrel of his rifle, and never once turned to see what might be going on behind him.

Kerwick raised his rifle, and aimed. But the barrel perceptibly wavered, and after an instant of hesitation he lowered the piece. He drew a long breath, aimed again, and then — *then*, with a convulsive jerk, he pulled the trigger.

At the crack of the rifle a little spray of glittering snow spurted up into the sunlight, just beyond the right edge of the target. The strain had been too heavy. Kerwick's last and all important shot had gone wide! A small, red flag was raised before the face of the target. Slowly, mockingly it was waved to and fro. "Miss," said the scorer softly, as he chalked down the fatal zero.

Pollard glanced quickly at the unlucky

captain, and then settled into position for firing. Kerwick laughed weakly, and faced about, to walk away. But suddenly he stopped, turned from the sympathizing group behind the firing point, and fixed his gaze upon the targets; for he had become aware that the muscles around his mouth were twitching, and that — because of the glaring snow, perhaps — his eyes were being blinded by a hot gush of tears.

There came a sharp report. Pollard's last bullet was speeding its way across the two hundred yards of snow. And in a moment the white disk crept into sight — *but not on Pollard's target !* Bullseye though the shot was, it could be scored only as a miss.

" Da' — thunderation ! " yelled Pollard, giving an exhibition of realistic acting sufficiently fine to have made Salvini faint dead away, could he have seen it. " Oh, glory ! I'm on the wrong target — and there goes the blooming old cup ! Kerwick's score outranks. What luck ! Oh, what *infernal* luck ! "

There was a roar from the crowd. The knot of excited watchers did not need to be reminded of the rule that, in the case of an absolute tie, the winning score is the one in which the ranking shots lie nearest towards the end. Half the officers sought relief for their feelings by thumping Kerwick upon the back. The other half, among whom little Poore was more than conspicuous, piled themselves upon Pollard. And it was a long time before anybody heard Kerwick protesting that, whatever else he might have won, the cup was Pollard's, because of a clause in the half-forgotten deed of gift by which the donor was barred from winning his own trophy.

" Why did I do it ? " said Pollard later, when reproached for the brilliancy of his shooting in the earlier part of his score. " Well, you see, I just had to. Old Kerwick wouldn't have half enjoyed his winning if he hadn't been pushed for the place. Besides, if I'd shot much worse, that child Poore would have gobbled the cup, which never would have done. For I wanted that myself. But I felt like a beast, just the same, when poor old Kerwick broke down, after he'd started a lead mine in the snow with that last bullet of his."

OFFICIALLY REPORTED.

OFFICIALLY REPORTED.

THIS tale already has been in print. Browning, of the *Herald*, Rodman, of the *Globe*, and Major Larry, of The Third, were jointly responsible for its first appearance. But inasmuch as it was printed in the papers, and since things that see the light in that way speedily are forgotten — unless, to the confusion of those who first perpetrated them, they happen to be available for resurrection in deadly parallel columns — it has seemed good to rescue it from the oblivion of last year's dusty files.

Major Larry, it will be remembered, is the young gentleman whom Captain Tom Stearns, of *A* Company, once upon a time appointed "Company Kid" of his command. How Larry afterwards demonstrated the wisdom of the captain's selection, and how he won promotion to the position for which his soul yearned — the post of honor at the front of the big bass-drum — already has been told. In fact, since Major Larry numbers his friends and acquaintances by the hundred, he needs no farther introduction.

It was two weeks after the regimental autumn manœuvres, and twenty minutes after *recall* had sounded on a certain drill night. The adjutant threaded his way along the swarming corridors of the big armory, climbed a flight of oaken stairs, and turned in at the doorway of *A's* quarters. In the captain's room he found Major Larry, industriously plying a whisk broom upon a braided fatigue-jacket.

" Where's Stearns ? " demanded the adjutant, halting upon the threshold.

Larry promptly brought his heels together, tucked the jacket under his left arm, and smartly raised his right hand, brush and all, to his forehead. " Cap'n Stearns ? " said he. " He's flew."

" Humph ! " grunted the adjutant. " The captain's *flew*, eh ? And his report's ten days over-due ! "

" W'at's de report dat's missin' ? " anxiously inquired Larry.

The adjutant turned and looked down

upon his questioner. "Oh, it's not a matter of life-and-death importance," said he; "only Captain Stearns ought to have sent in a written account of his company's part in the manœuvres, and I should have had it long ago."

"I was wid *A*," said the boy. "W'at's de matter wid *me* reportin' ? "

The adjutant paused and considered. Major Larry is noted for keen observation of men and things, and his command of words, such as they are, is a source of joy to all at headquarters. The adjutant decided accordingly. "What's the matter indeed!" said he, starting towards the colonel's room. "Come along with me, Major. We'll make this report a verbal one."

In the colonel's private office a coal fire was glowing in the open grate. Before it sat the chief, with Browning and Rodman, the two "war correspondents," who had dropped in to see if anything of interest in regimental matters was about to happen. Everybody in the service knows Browning and Rodman, and knows them, moreover, collectively; because, as a rule, where one of them is found, there also is to be found the other. What would the annual tour of camp duty be without their presence? And how, but for them, would the great and careless Public be kept from forgetting the very existence of that modest institution, the volunteer service?

"Did you get that report?" asked the colonel, looking up as the adjutant and Major Larry entered.

"No, sir," replied the adjutant. "Captain Stearns is compelled to ask for an extension of time. But I've done the next best thing. Here's Major Larry Callahan, the captain's chief of staff, who has kindly volunteered to report in person on the operations of *A* Company."

At the adjutant's opening words the colonel frowned, but, as he finished, the frown gave way to a very broad smile. Larry neither frowned nor smiled, but stood attention, awaiting orders. He was very much in earnest, feeling that his patron, the delinquent captain, was in a bad box, from which it was his duty to extricate him.

Rodman leaned over towards his fellow journalist, and said something in a low tone, at the same time placing a coin upon his knee, concealed by his outspread hand.

" Heads," said Browning, nodding assent to the proposition that had been made.

" Guess again ! " said Rodman, uncovering the silver piece ; " it's tails. This is *my* story." And he quietly drew a note-book from his pocket.

" Well ? " said the colonel, turning towards Larry.

" It's be'n dis way wid de cap'n," said the boy ; " he isn't had much time since de battle, an' to-night he was called out o' town sudden. I jus' got a cab for'm to hustle to de ten-t'irty express. But I c'n report w'at *A* done, if youse want it right off, jus' as well's de cap'n could. 'Cause I was dere, see ? An' I didn't have nuttin' on me mind 'ceptin' to catch on to w'at was happenin'. It was diffrunt wid de cap'n : he was busy wid bot' han's, tryin' to keep de boys from blowin' de heads off'n 'emselves."

" I see," said the colonel. " But you should have been with the drum corps, Larry. What brought you in with *A* ?"

" Well," said Major Larry in some confusion, " t'ings was terruble slow in de drummin' department. We wasn't in de fight, you know, sir, an' I didn't feel like I was learnin' nuttin' 'bout war, a-sittin' down in de shade an' listenin' to de fellies tell yarns dat was grey headed w'en Noah was yachtin' in de ark. So w'en de drum major started in to get off de rattiest ches'nut o' de season, I oozed out o' sight behin' a big tree, an' from dat I skinned across to anodder one, an' den I sneaked it, t'rough de brush an' over de fields, to where *A* was posted."

"H'm!" muttered the colonel, frowning darkly. "How long is it, Adjutant, since we've had to have a regimental court-martial?"

"I didn't mean to do nuttin' wrong, sir!" said Larry hastily. "I wasn't no use where I was, an' I t'ought p'raps I c'd be some help to de cap'n if I happened over dat way. I didn't t'ink de drum major needed me any longer, sir. An' he didn't say I couldn't go. Hones'!"

"Well, you can thank your lucky stars that I didn't catch you away from your post," said the colonel grimly. "This time I'll overlook the breach of discipline on account of your extreme youth, but you'll do well to be careful in the future. And now go on with your report."

The adjutant quietly slipped out of the room, going in the direction of the staff office. He was back again in an instant, and soon after he had seated himself, Langforth, the paymaster, and Woodleigh, Q. M., casually put in an appearance and took possession of a couple of chairs near the door.

" I — I don' know," said Larry hesitatingly, in response to the colonel's command, "jus' exackly how to begin. I was dere, for a fac', an' seen de whole scrap — but I aint used to makin' reports."

" You'll begin," said the colonel, slowly and impressively, "by describing the *terrain* — "

" *W'at's* dat?" interrupted Larry most respectfully.

"It means the lay of the land," said the colonel. " You'll describe to us the lay of the land. Then you'll state the disposition of the troops engaged. And then you'll tell what those troops did, paying particular attention to the operations of *A* Company. Go on."

Major Larry fumbled for an instant with

one of the shining brass buttons of his blue blouse, then stiffened his back, cleared his throat, saluted, and began his account of the battle.

"I have de honor to report," said he, " dat de follerin' t'ings took place, sir, jus' two weeks ago yesterd'y, w'ich was Toosd'y.

"First, 'bout de lay o' de lan': it lain dis way. Dere was a big hayin' field, shaped somet'in' like a big piece o' pie wid a big bite tooken out'n one end of it — dat is, out'n de small end o' de wedge. De roundin' edge o' de field, same's de part o' de pie dat comes nex' de rim o' de plate, was composed of a river. Dis was 'bout two foot deep, an' it couldn't be forded across by militia, 'count o' de danger o' wettin' pants, w'ich is State propity. So's dis part o' de battle-field was dead-safe. See?"

Rodman desisted for a moment from inscribing distorted fish-hooks in his note-book, and glanced towards the colonel. The chief was vigorously twisting his grey moustache in a vain attempt to maintain his official composure.

"Nex' dat roundin' edge," continued Larry with his eyes fixed upon the golden eagle surmounting the regimental color which occupied one corner of the room, "come a straight edge. Dat was a road, an' where it joined de roundin' edge was at a bridge 'cross de river. Den come de point w'ich had be'n bit off. W'at youse might call de mout'ful was a sort o' mixed-up mess o' bushes an' trees.

"Dis 'counts for de crust edge, an' one side, an' de bit place o' de piece o' pie. De side dat's lef' was made by t'ree little hills, wid an ol' stone wall runnin' up an' down along de tops of 'em, like de stripe on a sergeant's trowsies. An' dat was de way in w'ich de lay o' de lan' lain."

Langforth rose and stepped over to the corner in which stood the black-board on whose surface have been worked out so many problems in regimental strategy. He made a few rapid passes with the chalk, and there came into being a map of a range of three low hills, looking down across a triangular field towards a highway, and flanked on one side by a river, on the other by a patch of scrubby woodland.

"Dat's de stuff!" commented Larry approvingly, as this example of topographical art took form. "'Twas *jus'* like dat."

"Now," said the paymaster to the boy. "you can put in your troops."

Larry took the crayon in his unwilling fingers, and doubtfully advanced upon the black-board. He often had seen officers lay off the broad white lines denoting the positions of battalions and companies, but he was not quite sure that he could perform the feat himself. However, he was not going to give up without a trial, and so, bracing himself for the effort, he slowly and carefully scraped the chalk across the black surface before him.

"De sec'nd battalion was de enermy," said he, after he had chalked the map to his satisfaction. "Dat is, we was de enermy o' de first an' t'ird battalions. Dey, o' course, was *our* enermy. *G* was on dis hill, *H* was on de middle 'un, an' *L* was on de one at de lef'. *A* was deplored as skirmishers."

"'*Deplored* as skirmishers!'" said the colonel softly. "Wonder how Stearns would like that bit of description."

. "Oh, I mos' forgot tellin' 'bout de disposition o' de troops," said Major Larry, suddenly recalling one of the chief's requirements. "Near's I c'd make out, de disposition o' most of 'em was fine. Our fellies was disposed to knock de stuffin' out'n de enermy, an' if it hadn't be'n for de cap'n and de lieutenants we'd have started a private dead-yard down in our corner w'en *K*'s boys come chargin' inter de woods.

"An' dis brings me to de report o' de share *A* took in de purceedin's. Dis is w'at *A* done: de odder t'ree comp'nies was squattin' down a-top o' de t'ree little hills, an' *A* was shooken out in a skirmish line, down 'long by de bridge, to make it unhealt'y for de furriners w'en dey come promenadin' ahead to cross de river.

"Majur Pollard, he comes ridin' down from de hills, an. he says, 'Cap'n Stearns,' says he, 'w'en you're drove back from dis position, youse'll fall back down de road here, an' take y'r command into de cover o' de woods on our right flank dere,' pointin' at it wid his sword. 'Dat's a strong position,' says he, 'an' de div'l himself couldn't drive yer out'n it if dis was really bizness. By doin' dis youse'll purtec' our flank from bein' turned, an' at de same time'll uncover de front of us, so's dat we c'n play fire-works wid de enermy's advance. See?' An' de cap'n said he seen, an' later he done so."

Here Larry armed himself with the long, tapering pointer, and then proceeded with his narrative. "W'en I come up to re-enforce de comp'ny, de enemy was jus' marchin' down to shove us away from de bridge. It was a dandy sight! De two battalions looked bigger'n brigades, an' de colors was wavin', an' —" here Larry was caught by a sudden inspiration — "an de colonel was lookin' elegant, on a big, white hoss, an' —" with a second inspired utterance — "de newspaper men was hustlin' 'roun' an' gettin' on to everyt'ing!"

This bit of spirited description was most favorably received. The personages mentioned bowed their acknowledgments, while Langforth and Woodleigh and the adjutant applauded generously, and shouted in chorus, "*Hear! Hear!*"

"I'd make me oat'," said Major Larry, thus encouraged, "dat dis is de bes' regiment in de State. W'y, de odder regiments isn't got no use at all for us! Dey isn't in it wid us, an' anybody wid bot' eyes shut c'd tumble to dat. See?"

"You're not disputed, Major Callahan," said the colonel, clasping his hands across his chest. "Proceed with your report."

"Well, de enermy kep' moggin' along down to de river," said the boy obediently, "an' w'en dey was gettin' good an' handy de cap'n assembled de comp'ny, an' sung out, 'Now youse'll all set y'r sights at t'ree hunderd, an' every popper's boy of youse must take aim careful. For de nex' act on de programme,' says he, 'is goin' to be a volley exercuted by de full strengt' of all de artists in de troupe.'"

"Hold up for a minute, Larry," broke in the colonel, when this truly remarkable order was quoted. "Were those Captain Stearns' exact words?"

"Well, no-o, sir," admitted Major Larry. "P'raps dat aint jus' w'at he said, but it's w'at he was gettin' at, anyhow. He 'xplained to 'em dat if 'twas truly fightin', 'stead o' bein' de imitation, he'd keep 'em all under his t'umb, an' not let 'em give no exhibition of a lead shower-bat', by squirtin' bullets all over de lan'scape at deir own sweet conveniences. In odder words, he give 'em to understan' dat, w'en it come to firin' by comp'ny, w'at he said *went !*"

"Perfectly proper," said the colonel, who is a thorough believer in the virtues of controlled fire. "Perfectly proper. I noticed that Stearns handled his practice very well when he was at the bridge."

"We done t'ree or four volleys," continued Larry, "but it was sort o' discouragin' bizness, 'cause we didn't seem to see no corpses carted off, an' all we could do didn't seem like it was hurtin' de enermy's feelin's much. So w'en dey kep' gettin' closer an' closer, we seen dat dey was boun' to waltz over de bridge, spite of us, an' de cap'n come to de conclusion dat he'd done all dat a brave man could to stan' 'em off. W'ich bein' so, he marched de comp'ny off an' fell back down de road, leavin' de premises clear for de t'ree comp'nies on de hills to show w'at dey was good for.

"Well, we was marched down de road, an' formed up in line among de trees, where it was cool an' shady. An' den we got de chance to see sights. De attackin' battalions come swarmin' over dat bridge like a big mob o' de unemployed, an' begun to push forward for de hills, an' de rifles started goin' *poppety-poppety-pop!* An' dere we was sittin' like an audyence in de gallery, takin' in de whole show for nuttin'. But we wasn't quite out of it, for all of a sudd'n de cap'n says, ' Here's w'ere we wipes out dat fool flank comp'ny !' An' wid dat he has us plug a volley square into 'em.

" Now, dat was like yellin' ' *Rats!* ' in t'rough de door of a Chinee laundry ! O' course dey wasn't nobody killed by dat volley, 'cause de odder fellies was too far off to be hit by de wads. But de effec' was queer, an' youse c'n bet y'r sweet natyral dat was de size of it !

" *K* was de comp'ny dat happened to be on dat flank, an' w'en we plunked dat volley at 'em dey seemed like dey was excited. I guess dey t'ought we was gettin' too funny wid 'm, for dey swung back so's to be facin' our way, an' den begun poppin' at us for all dey was wort'.

" But *dat* never fazed us, 'cause we knew dat deir rifles didn't have no slugs in 'em, an' dat we was pretty well out o' sight amongst de trees. An' besides all dat, we also was aware dat de fellies in *K* couldn't shoot well enough to hit a mountain if 'twas pushed up to 'em on rollers. Huh! most o' de men in *K* handles deir rifles like dey was crowbars, an' a flock of elerphants flyin' low c'd sail over deir heads widout no occasion for worryin'!" This was taking a mean advantage. Larry had a personal grievance against *K* Company, and sought revenge by improving the opportunity to slander that command in his report.

"Now, after t'ings had be'n goin' on in dis way for a little w'ile," continued Larry, "I seen a chance to tally one for our side. W'at I mean is dis — Say, d'youse know Hickey, dat big, fat-headed corp'ral in *K?*"

The colonel was compelled to disclaim the acquaintance of any such person. The adjutant, however, whose knowledge of the regimental *personnel* was necessarily more extended, came to time promptly with an affirmative nod.

"Well, he's a dam' chump!" said Larry, with emphasis. "Oh, 'xcuse me!" he hastily added, as it dawned upon him that his language had been a trifle unparliamentary; "I didn't mean to say jus' dat. But he's a reg'lar galvanized gazaboo, an' nuttin' else. See? Him an' his gang had fun wid me, one night last camp, tossin' me in a blanket, an' I've be'n layin' low for'm ever since dat. I'm like an Injun — 'I never forgets de face of a foe ! ' " This evidently was a quotation from some modern master-piece of literature, and Larry delivered it most impressively.

" But dis aint tellin' w'at I seen." Here the boy picked up the chalk, and made a few additional marks upon the map of the battle-ground. " It was like dis," said he, stepping back a pace and resting one hand easily upon his hip, while he gracefully wielded the pointer with the other; " de fellies in *K* was in plain sight, out in de sun, an' I was here, 'way down at de right o' de line. See ? " He indicated his own position by means of the pointer. " Dey was a tree dere, growin' out'n a crack in a big rock, an' I was camped down behin' de whole bizness, blazin' away for glory, an' makin' every shot tell, w'en I seen — "

" Eh ? " said the colonel. " What's that ? What were *you* doing with a rifle ? "

" Shootin', sir," said Larry briefly.

" Yes, so it would appear," said the colonel. " But how came you to be armed ? "

" W'y, Smit'y de Invalid — he's de felly, y'know, dat's always tryin' to sneak off from doin' any duty — he'd tol' me dat he wasn't feelin' jus' well, an' I'd tooken his rifle to hold for'm w'ile he went off huntin' for a drink o' cold water. He didn't give me no ca'tridges, but I'd jollied de boys out'n a pocketful, an' had organized meself into a Mosby gorilla. De cap'n, o' course, he didn't know nuttin' 'bout all dis, or he'd a-be'n wild. Dat's de reason I was 'way off dere to de right — to keep out'n de cap'n's way. See?"

The colonel silently nodded. Apparently he "saw." Major Larry, having given this satisfactory explanation of matters, resumed the delivery of his interrupted report.

"I tol' yer dat I seen a promisin' openin' for stratergy," he said; "an' dis was it: me bein' off to de right of *A* brought me facin' de lef' flank o' *K*, an' *who* should I discover opposite o' me but dat same Hickey! Now, seein' Hickey so convenient set me to t'inkin'.

"'Hickey, me ol' sporty,' says I to meself, 'I'm on y'r trail. Youse once had fun, heaps o' fun, a-joshin' me,' says I, 'but dis is de time I'm comin' back at you,' says I. 'Dat's de kind of a Reuben dat *I* am,' says I. An' wid dat I fired two blank ca'tridges at'm, aimin' careful at his stummick, so's to ease me min'. Den I hid me rifle in de scrub, so's de cap'n wouldn't see me wid it, an' slid along back to de nearest boys on de right of *A*.

" Big Jonesey was dere, an' McKenzie, an' Schultz — all of 'em aimin' an' firin' like dey was expectin' to put medals onto deir dress. coats t'icker'n de scales on a fish. Dere wasn't an officer widin hearin', bot' de lieutenants bein' off to de centre consultin' 'bout somet'in' wid de cap'n. W'ich was lucky.

" '*Whis-st, boys!*' says I careful, wavin' me arm 'round me head to signal 'em to rally up to me. Dey seen dat I meant somet'in', an' closed up to-wards me. 'Sa-ay, youse t'ink you're doin' fancy work, a-shootin' holes in nuttin', doesn't youse?' says I, w'en dey'd assembled on me. 'Well, if youse'll quit y'r foolishness an' foller me,' I says, 'youse'll wear di'mon's. Come on lively, 'fore de lieutenant gets back to miss yer,' says I.

" Well, dey gives me a look, an' den dey looks back t'wards de comp'ny an' sees dat de chances is dat dey'll not be missed for a little w'ile, an' den de four of us takes a quiet sneak off t'rough de shrubb'ry.

" ' Now jus' listen to me w'ile I gurgle,' I says, w'en we'd got to de place w'ere me

rifle was hid. 'D'youse see dat phernome-
num out dere in de horizon? Well, dat bird
o' paradise,' I says, 'is Hickey, Corp'ral
Hickey, o' *K* Comp'ny.'

"'I want to know if it is!' says Jonesey.
'An' have youse pulled us out here to give
us dat important information! I'm t'inkin'
o' breakin' y'r back, Larry,' says he, 'an' I
would, too, if 'twasn't for losin' yer de job o'
luggin' de big drum.'

"'Is dat *so?*' says I, dodgin' a swipe he
made at me head. 'S'posin' youse wait for
me to get t'rough! I'm not talkin' to fill up
no fonygraft; I'm talkin' *war*.'

"'Leaf'm alone,' says Schultz, 'an' see vat
he hass upon dot gr-reat mindt off his.' An'
Jonesey, he lef' me alone.

"'Yes, dat's Corp'ral Hickey,' says I, in-
dicatin' me objective again wid me rifle. 'I
know'm easy by de size of his ears. An' if
youse fellies isn't all stiffs, we c'n capture
him alive. W'at d'youse say?' I says.
'Are youse mugs wid me, or agin me?'

"McKenzie allowed· dat 'twould be sport
if we could scoop in Hickey, an' Schultz was
agreeable to de scheme, so den I 'xplained
w'at I wanted 'em to do, an' we started in on

de conspiracy. An' all dis time, mind youse, de battle was goin' on hot an' heavy. But we wasn't mindin' nobody's funeral 'ceptin' ours — an' I was de undertaker!

"Dis is w'at I done wid de boys : I posted 'em behin' bushes an' trees, right up close to de edge o' de woods, but so far from w'ere de flank of *A* lain dat nobody ever'd catch on to deir bein' dere. An' den I give me rifle to McKenzie, an' strolled out into de field an' over 'cross t'wards de lef' o' *K*.

"W'en I got widin 'bout fifty yards o' Mister Hickey, bein' kind o' quarterin'n a' off to one side of 'm, I sings out an' says 'Does yoore face pa-ain youse, Hickey?' I says. 'I notices dat it kind o' gets twisted out o' shape in aimin'. By de way youse wrinkles up dat lef' eye I should t'ink dat one o' y'r lights was went out,' I says. Dat seemed to catch de boys in Hickey's squad, an' dey give'm de gran' laff.

"'Go chase yerself off'n de field, Larry,' says Hickey, answerin' me back. 'Dis aint no place for kids. 'Tisn't safe for youse 'round w'ere I am. I'm feelin' dryer'n a covered bridge, an' 'twouldn't take much to make me catch yer an' drink y'r blood.'

"'*Ya-as, yer would!*' says I, t'umbin' me nose to'm. 'Catch nawthin'! Youse couldn't catch a cooky at a cake-walk!'

"'I'll give yer jus' t'irty secon's to clear out in,' says Hickey, gettin' kind o' looney, 'cause de squad was snickerin' again, 'an' if y'aint disappeared by dat time, I'll collar yer, an' roll yer up into a small an' bloody bundle, an' stuff yer inter me haversack for safe keepin'.'

"'Huh! w'at youse say cuts no ice wid me!' says I, scornful. 'It's clean nutty dat youse are. See? Holdin' down a slab in de morgue's all youse c'n do graceful. Sure!'

"Dat was. jus' a little bit more'n Hickey was prepared to stan'. 'Here, hang on to me rifle,' says he, handin' it over to de neares' man o' de squad, 'an' watch me capture de firs' prisoner o' de campaign.' An' wid dat he gives a proud leer, an' makes a break for me.

"'Some o' youse hol' de watch on us,' I sings out. 'Dis is for de amachoor sprintin' rekid!' An' off I starts for de brush, towin' me victim along behin' me.

"Oh, 'twas hot stuff! At firs' I was 'fraid dat some of his officers would catch onto'm

an' call'm back; but de smoke was driftin'
off our way, an' we was travellin' away from
de flank o' de battalion, an' so nobody paid
no 'tention to us 'cept a few o' de boys down
at dat end.

"Well, I kep' humpin' for all I was wort', an'
Hickey, he was after me for all *he* was wort',
an' fin'lly we strikes cover at 'bout de same
time. I makes a flyin' dive inter de bushes,
like a rabbit wid de shakin' jim-jams, an'
Hickey shoots'mself in after me — an' lands
up against de muzzle o' Jonesey's rifle!"

"'Halt!' sings out Jonesey, 'an' surrender,
you red-handed cut-t'roat!' An' Hickey halts
—prompt, too. But 'stead o'. surrenderin',
he turned an' started to take a travel back for
de open. An' jus' den Schultz, he rose up
out'n de eart' on de one side of'm, an' Mc-
Kenzie, he surrounded 'm on de odder side, an'
den poor Hickey seen dat his goose was
cooked.

"'T'row'm down, boys,' I says. An' dey
t'run'm down, an' de place w'ere dey happened to t'run'm was boggy, so's dat w'en
he rose up he looked like he hadn't shooken
hands wid a piece o' soap for more'n a mont'.

"'Boys, it's me sorrerful dooty,' I says,

'to tell yer dat Hickey's drinkin' again.'
An' den I tol'm w'at he'd said 'bout capturin'
me an' drinkin' me blood. An' dey was
astonished an' shocked.

"'Is dis civerlized war?' says McKenzie,
glarin' at de pris'ner. 'You're worse dan a
Dahomey cannib'l — scarin' de life out'n dis
innercent child! Shall we give 'm quarter?'
he says, turnin' to de odder fellies.

"'I've got a few t'ousand in me clodes,'
I says, like I was considerin', 'but I aint got
no quarter for *him*. Away wid 'm!' I says.

"'Dammit!' says Hickey, growin' excited,
'can't youse quit y'r foolin'? I mus' be
gettin' back to de comp'ny or I'll be losin'
me stripes!'

"'Hear de hardened vilyun cursin' w'en
deat' stares'm in de eye!' says McKenzie,
holdin' up his hands wid horror. 'Oh, Hickey,
Hickey, you're in danger o' losin' de number o'
y'r mess — den w'y worry 'bout a little t'ing
like a pair o' miser'ble corp'ral's stripes?'

"'Boys,' I says, 'I pity dis poor mug.
S'posin' we fin' out how he's feelin' 'bout dis
time?' An' I turned t'wards de pris'ner.
'Hickey,' I says, 'are youse ever goin' to
preside over anodder blanket-tossin' conven-

tion — I mean, one wid *me* in it?' An' he swore dat he hones' wouldn't.

"'Higky,' asks Schultz, 'vill you dot pecos off dis affair dere shall no hart veelin' pe?' An' Hickey said dat dere shouldn't.

"'Hickey,' says McKenzie, w'en it come his turn at de bat, 'if you're lucky 'nough to come out alive at de end o' dis awful day o' strife will youse remember dat odder people 'sides y'rself has t'roats — w'ich needs occasional wettin'?' An' Hickey give his word dat he'd set 'em up for de crowd w'en we got back to town.

"'Dis all bein' so,' says Jonesey, 'an' no objection bein' made, we'll spare y'r wort'-less life. But we're under oat' to do our full duty by de Commonwealt' for a term o' t'ree years, an' so we can't let yer go. Private McKenzie on de right, Private Schultz on de lef', de pris'ner betwixt youse — *fall in!*' says he. An' dey fell in, an' started back t'wards de comp'ny, wid Hickey a-kickin' himself for a t'underin' jackuss, an' me a-follerin', t'umpin' meself wid joy.

"Well, we comes back to de comp'ny, an' I makes a break for de head o' de percession — 'cause 'twas *my* entertainment, y' know —

an' w'en de fellies sees us marchin' up, dey sets up a yell, for dey all knows Hickey. An' w'en we gets to de cap'n I salutes an' says, 'Cap'n, here's a spy,' I says. 'W'at'll we do wid'm?'

"Cap'n Stearns, he looked Hickey all over, an' seen de dirt on'm, an' says, 'Whew! he looks like he'd be'n huntin' for trouble an' foun' it! Are dey diggin' a mine under us, or w'at? Take'm away,' he says, 'an' play de hose on'm an' don't bodder me wid'm.' An' he had to laff.

"But he didn't get no time for a real *good* laff, 'cause jus' den de enemy begun to charge us, an' he had his han's full keepin' de boys from fightin' in earnest. For our fellies wasn't goin' to let *K* walk on deir necks. But 'twas 'gainst orders for bayonets to be crossed, an' so we played dat we was captured. But we wasn't, all de same, for if't had b'en really *war* we'd have kep' a coroner's jury busy for a week sortin' out de remains o' *K*.

"An' dat, sir," said Major Larry, facing towards the colonel with a final salute, "near's I c'n remember, is w'at *A* done, two weeks ago yesterd'y, at de right o' Major Pollard's line o' battle."

The colonel brought out a half-dollar. "Larry," said he, handing it to the boy, "we all are greatly indebted to you for your excellent and most technical report. For my own part, I can truthfully say that I've learned a great deal about grand strategy. You are excused, with the thanks of all present."

Larry left the room with the step of a grenadier. Rodman closed his note-book with a snap, saying softly, "That'll be good for two columns." There was an instant of awed silence. And then the colonel turned to the adjutant, and said, "Hereafter, Charley, there'll be two reports made of anything that *A* may be concerned in — one written, and one oral. That's a standing order. *See?*"

Rodman's notes worked up to two columns and a half of the next day's *Globe*, and for a second time Major Larry Callahan found himself locally famous. What Captain Tom Stearns said when his eye fell upon the marked copy of the paper which was thoughtfully mailed to him by the adjutant, is not upon record. But it is a fact that he has been more than prompt, of late, in the matter of forwarding required reports.

SPECIAL ORDERS, NO. 49.

THEY call it the incurable ward. In coming down the corridor one sees above its doorway, upon the blank, white wall, a plain, black letter *A*. It almost seems as though the painter had thought to transcribe there, "All hope abandon" — and then had relented, after outlining the initial letter of the grisly legend. Perhaps he well might have finished his work, for those who enter that quiet room are borne thither because their days are nearly numbered.

On that afternoon there was but one patient in Ward *A*. He seemed content to lie motionless, watching with drowsy, half-closed eyes the play of a stray shaft of sunlight upon the snowy counterpane. Beside him, steadily swinging a fan, sat a white-robed nurse. The long June day was wearing slowly on towards its ending.

In through the casement to the westward there came a soft breath of flower-scented air. The nurse felt its caress upon her cheek, and laid aside her fan. Then, with a little sigh of relief, she rose from her chair, and quietly stole over to the window for a moment's glance out into the garden which lay below.

She was standing there when her trained ear caught the sound of a restless movement upon the cot. " A glass of water, please," murmured the sick man, as she turned and came quickly towards him.

" Thank you," said he, after a long, grateful draught from the glass which she had held to his lips. " I must be a terrible nuisance to you. But," he added, in a lower tone, "it'll not be for much longer, please God!"

" *Sh-h!* " said the nurse, reprovingly. " You mustn't say that. I can't see, I'm sure, why it should be thought that nurses are intended more for ornament than use. Not," with a smile, " but that we're flattered by that view of the situation."

" But really and truly," she went on, picking up the fan, " we should grow terribly tired of the monotony if it weren't for the relief that comes from doing these little things."

"I suppose I must believe you," said the sick man, smiling faintly in his turn. "And if — 'really and truly' — it will serve to break the monotony, I'll venture to ask you to do me one more favor. About that packet of trinkets that I —"

"Oh, how stupid of me!" exclaimed the nurse, hastily rising from her chair. "The superintendent sent them in while you were taking your nap." With the swift, noiseless step of one long trained in hospital service she crossed the room, and took from the mantel a small package. "Here they are," said she. "Shall I take them out for you?"

At his nod of assent she deftly untied the faded blue ribbon with which the packet was secured, removed the tissue-paper covering, and brought to light a jewel-case, in which lay three military decorations — the badge of the Loyal Legion, the plain, bronze star of the Grand Army, and the enamelled Maltese cross of the old 19th Army Corps.

One by one she laid the medals upon the thin hand feebly outstretched over the white coverlid, and for a moment the sick man's tired eyes kindled as he gazed upon them. But the feeble hand relaxed, the eyes quickly became dim again. "Ah, well," he said, a bit huskily, "I'm through — through with all that now. And I've no son — there's no one to care — no one to whom I can leave these things. You'll see that some one pins them on my breast when — when I'm carried out?"

"Yes," said the nurse, gathering up the medals as she spoke, "I'll be very careful about having it done." And then she added quietly, "I'll attend to it myself."

"I'm wofully helpless," said the man upon the cot apologetically; "may I trouble you to hand me the photograph?"

The nurse drew from beneath his pillow a faded and worn morocco case, opened it, and handed it to him. Then she turned away and made pretence of busying herself about some little matter, while her charge looked long and wistfully upon the picture of a woman's face that smiled back at him from its resting place within the leathern frame.

The sick man sighed, but not unhappily. A look of peace came upon his worn face, and a smile — a wonderfully tender smile — hovered about his lips.

" Will you put the medals under my pillow?" said he, as the nurse came towards the bed. "Thank you. Really, you've been very kind to me. I'd like to tell you how grateful I am for it all — but may be I needn't. My mind's quite at rest now : those letters that you wrote for me settled the last of my worries. And now I'm not sure — I think — think that perhaps I could sleep again for a little while." He wearily turned his head to one side, resting it upon the palm of his hand. And within the hand, pressed close against his cheek, lay the photograph in its worn and faded case.

The nurse smoothed out the pillow, passed her hand gently over the iron-grey hair that clustered thickly above his forehead, and taking her place by the bedside, once more began to swing the fan slowly to and fro.

In the great, white room the shadows deepened as the sun went down. The sick man was breathing regularly, but very lightly. He had fallen asleep. Once the silent watcher saw his lips move, and caught the sound of murmured words : then all was still again. The fan swung slowly back and forth — still more slowly — and then it stopped.

The world outside seemed very beautiful in the June twilight, and the confinement, by contrast, became doubly irksome. The nurse slipped quietly over to the open window. She was standing there when the house surgeon came briskly into the room. " S-sh!" said she, turning at the sound of the footsteps, and raising a warning hand. " He's asleep."

But the surgeon already was standing beside the cot. He gave one keen glance at the form lying before him, and placed his hand over the heart. Then he straightened up and turned towards the nurse. His face had become grave. " Yes," said he, in answer to the look of anxious inquiry; " yes, he's asleep. I hadn't looked for this before tomorrow," he went on quietly, " but he's — he's asleep, as you say."

Dimness had come with the failing light, but it was not so dark that the doctor and the nurse could not see upon the dead man's face the calm smile of perfect peace. " See," whispered the nurse, gently drawing the photograph from its resting place — and as she held the picture towards her companion she gave a little sob. " Yes, I see," said the surgeon, softly. "I know his story." And then in a lower tone he added, "He's asleep at last. *God send him rest!*"

It was nearing nine o'clock. Colonel Elliott glanced at his watch, and then leaned back in his chair with the comfortable consciousness that his evening's work was over. One by one he had gone through the pile of papers that he had found upon his desk. He had written, "Respectfully forwarded, approved," upon each in its turn, and now they were ready to go to the adjutant, to be entered up and sent along upon their sluggish travels "through channels."

The colonel gathered the scattered documents into a bunch, snapped a rubber band about them, and then called, "Orderly!"

"Take these papers to the adjutant," said the chief, as a soldier stepped promptly into the room, with his hand at his cap. "Then find Major Pollard, and say to him, with my compliments, that I'd like him to report to me here."

The orderly saluted, and disappeared. The colonel bit the tip from a cigar, lighted it, and then drew from his pocket a half dozen letters. Rapidly running through them, he picked out one, tossed it upon his desk, and then, letting his head fall back, he fixed his eyes upon the ceiling, and smoked away in thoughtful silence.

Along the broad corridors of the armory echoed the steady tramp of feet, the rattle of arms, and the sharp commands of the line officers, for it was a regular drill-night of The Third, and four of the regiment's twelve companies were at work in the great hall lying beyond the administrative rooms. Presently, above the hum of the other sounds, the colonel heard quick, firm footsteps approaching his door, and in a moment Major Pollard and Van Sickles, of the staff, came into the room.

"You sent for me, Colonel?" said the major, inquiringly.

"Yes," said the chief, adding, as Van Sickles made a motion as if to withdraw, "I'd like to have you stay, Van. I've something to tell that'll answer a question you once asked me."

Both drew up chairs. The colonel passed over his cigar case, and then said, "A year ago you fellows got me to talking, one night up in The Battery, about something that happened while I was out with the ' Old Regiment.' As I recall it, I told you a yarn about the resurrection of Bob Sheldon, and you, Van, asked me, when I'd finished, what had become of Bob since the war. Do you remember ? "

" Sheldon ? " said Van Sickles. " Oh, yes. He was the man that was brained by a splinter of shell, and afterwards came to time all right. Your old captain, wasn't he ? Yes, I remember."

" Well," said the colonel slowly, " I had a letter from him this morning — and he's dead."

" Not really ! " said Van Sickles, as the chief made this odd announcement. " Well, I'm sorry on your account, sir."

" He's dead, poor old Bob ! " said the colonel, resting his elbow upon the edge of his desk and letting his chin drop into the palm of his hand. " Yes, he's got his papers at last. And now, Van, I can take up the story that I left unfinished. It was incomplete then, but now the last chapter's been written."

" You've had the first of it already," went on the chief, settling back in his chair. " Here's the rest of it — and the last of it. You'll listen, too, Pollard.

" I've told you already, I think, that Bob Sheldon and I were the closest of friends. I stood up with him when he was married to his Nell — his 'little Nell' — the girl whose name came to his lips when he lay in delirium after the shell had struck him down. Poor little Nell — poor old Bob! Well, all the trouble's ended at last.

" The friendships that are made in active service are lasting ones. When the 'Old Regiment' came back, after doing its share of the work of hammering our erring brothers into a peaceful state, Bob was on the roster as major, and I'd been given his old company. But it never occurred to either of us, when off duty, that such a thing as rank had any existence. It was 'Bob' for him and 'Harry' for me, and he'd have thought me crazy if I'd addressed him as 'Major' except when I was at the head of my company.

" I'll be older than I am now before I forget the day that we were mustered out. We'd gone to the front with something over the full thousand : there were three hundred and sixty of us, rank and file, when we came home again. For we'd been a fighting regiment from start to finish, and the hard knocks of four long years had cut the original roll to ribbons. Those were the days when veteran regiments were allowed to dwindle down to skeletons, through battle and disease, while the recruits that should have been turned over to them to stop the gaps were herded together in one raw, half useless lump, given a fresh regimental number and a stand of colors bright and crisp from the shop, and then bundled off to where there was *fighting* to be done — and all because some ambitious politician felt that a pair of eagles would be becoming to his peculiar style of corpulent beauty.

"We had a royal welcome home. I needn't tell you what battles were gilded on the stripes of the old flag, because you know well enough the sort of record that we fellows made when cutting out the pace for you youngsters. We'd done our work, and we knew that we'd done it well, and we felt that the people knew it, too. And when we made our last march, that day, through the swarming streets, we took as rightfully ours the cheers that went up as the wreck of the 'Old Regiment' followed the faded colors home again.

" Then came the final breaking up; the
time when 'break ranks' meant that regimental line never would be formed again. I
remember how, for the last time, we presented
to the colors — the ragged, blood-streaked
scraps of silk whose worn folds told our
whole war story. Bob turned to me when
the tattered old things were being carried
away from us forever. His face was working, and — I doubt, though, if he knew it —
a big tear was rolling down each gaunt, sun-
burned cheek. I — well, I was sobbing like
a child, I'm not ashamed to say. So were
the boys at my back — God bless 'em !

" ' Bob,' says I, trying to swallow the lump
in my throat, ' Bob, old man, what's left for
us now ? ' He turned in his saddle and
looked across the parade to where a group of
white gowns — his Nell was there, with the
colonel's wife and a lot of other women —
had gathered to watch the last act in our
war drama. ' What's left ? ' says he, turning to
me again, ' What's left ? Why, *everything !* '
And though the tears still glistened at the
corners of his eyes, his face shone with the
light that has but one meaning.

" Well, we of the 'Old Regiment' shook

hands, and drifted back to our places in civil
life.   There are easier things than dropping
the customs of the service, and taking up the
monotony of everyday existence.   It came
hard at first, but we managed it somehow.

"Bob was married.   He wouldn't let a
week go by, after we were mustered out, before
he had that much of his career settled.   I
volunteered to stand by him to the last, and
he held me in reserve as best man until the
knot was safely tied.   It was a military wed-
ding.   Nearly all the officers of the 'Old
Regiment' were there.   It was a dingy looking lot of uniforms that gathered in the little
church, but the men inside the faded blue
coats were all right.

"It wasn't long before I followed Bob's example.   Then life ran on smoothly with us
both for a long stretch of years.   To be sure,
we missed the excitement of the old days;
but I'd come 'round to Bob's view of life, and
was willing to admit that there was a good
deal left to live for, after all.   There are several
queer things about war: one of 'em is the way
in which it teaches old soldiers to appreciate
the comfort of peace.

"Yes, life ran on smoothly for a time,"

repeated the colonel with a sigh; "and then came trouble, big trouble for poor Bob. He had one child, a boy. He was a bright, sturdy chap. Bob really believed that the world revolved 'round him. But just after he'd had his tenth birthday, he died.

"It was terribly rough! Bob had planned to send the youngster to 'The Point,' when the proper time came; and he'd talk to me by the hour of the pride he'd feel when he had a son in the service. 'Harry,' he'd say, when we'd be smoking our old pipes together, 'you and I were good enough soldiers according to our lights: we could fight just as nastily as though we'd been in the business for a lifetime. But when it came to the fine points of the profession, we weren't quite up to concert pitch; the fellows from 'The Point' scored on us then. Now, there's going to be another war some day. It's a long way ahead, and it's two to tuppence that we'll not be in it. But I want to feel that the name of Sheldon will be on some regiment's roster then — and I'm thinking that little Bob'll take care of that for me.'

"It was cruel work for poor Bob when we laid the little fellow away, and my heart went out to him in his trouble. But there was a heavier blow yet to fall. Two years after we'd buried the boy, I stood by Bob's side and gripped his arm while his wife's coffin was being lowered into the grave. My God! I learned then what despair meant. When all was over, Bob clung to me, and asked the question that I'd put to him on the day they took our old colors from us. 'Harry,' he said, almost with a groan, 'Harry, what's left for me now?' And before I could think of the words that I wanted, he answered his own question with, '*Nothing!*'

"And then I lost him for a time. He simply dropped everything and went away. For three years he was abroad, and from time to time I'd hear from him. But the letters were hopelessly unhappy, and I knew that he'd not recovered from the wrench that he'd got. Then came four months of silence.

"I was beginning to get alarmed at not hearing from him, when, one fearfully hot day in August, I looked up from my work, and saw him standing by the desk in my office. 'Pon my soul, I couldn't have been blamed for thinking that I saw his ghost! He was haggard and thin, and his eyes had a troubled, haunted look that made my heart ache for him.

" ' I'm back again,' he said, holding out his hand. 'It's hot, isn't it? I'm going to ask you a favor, Harry. The old house over in Cambridge has been closed ever since — ever since I went away, and I'm going there this afternoon : will you go with me ? '

" I hadn't lunched, but he seemed feverishly impatient to be off, and fairly dragged me along with him. We took a cab, and started on the long, hot ride. I did all the talking on the way: he sat silently by me, and his face wore a look that made me terribly uneasy.

" When we were nearly at the end of our ride I happened to catch sight of a doctor's sign upon the door of a house, and to my surprise I saw that it bore the name of the assistant surgeon of the 'Old Regiment.' A sudden idea came to me, and I made the cabman pull up, explaining to Bob that I'd a message to leave for a friend. I was pretty sure that he'd not notice anything : the look in his eyes told me that his mind was busy with something besides his surroundings.

" Running up to the door, I pulled the bell

in a way that meant business, and in a very short time I'd explained matters to the doctor. We agreed between us that the heat and the strain of coming back to the desolate home might work upon Bob in a fashion that, coupled with the effect of his old wound, would bring on bad results. So we arranged that the doctor should follow, in about a quarter of an hour, and drop in at Bob's house as if by accident. It was a clumsy sort of scheme, I must confess, but it was the best that I could think of under the circumstances.

"Bob and I drove on. When we reached the house, he tried to unlock the door, but his hand shook so pitifully that I took the key from him, and let him in. The house was hot and close, and the air musty with the damp of long disuse. It *was* a mournful home-coming, and I felt that it couldn't help doing harm of some sort to poor Bob.

"We went about from room to room. I opened a window here and there, for though the outside air was torrid anything seemed preferable to the closeness of those long untenanted walls. Bob moved in a dazed sort of way, as if he were walking in a dream.

I'd tried to find out if he had any definite object in coming, but he answered me incoherently, and I gave up my questioning.

"We'd been there for a full quarter of an hour when the door-bell rang. It sounded queerly, that tinkling peal in the silence of the deserted house. Bob jumped as if he'd been struck, when he heard the bell. 'What's that?' he said nervously.

"'I'll go to the door,' says I, knowing well enough what it meant. 'Thank you,' said Bob; 'if it isn't too much bother. I don't care about seeing any of the neighbors just yet. I'll run upstairs for a second, and you can call me when the coast's clear.'

"I opened the door, and there stood the doctor. 'Hello, Elliott!' he sang out, in a purposely loud voice, '*You* here? I happened to be passing, and noticed that the windows were open. Has the major come back?' He stepped into the hall, and I closed the door behind him. 'Yes, he turned up to-day,' said I, also very loudly and distinctly. 'He'll be glad to see you. Funny coincidence, your dropping in on us this way. Sort of regimental reunion, eh? We'll have to —'

" I stopped right there. A pistol shot rang out in one of the upper chambers, and after it came the sound of a heavy fall. ' God! we're too late,' gasped the doctor. But he rushed for the stairs without an instant's hesitation, and I tore up after him.

" Poor old Bob was lying on his face, in the room that had been his wife's. His old army revolver lay smoking beside him, where it had fallen when he dropped. The blood was streaming from his head, and the first horrified glance showed me that the track of the bullet almost exactly followed the scar left by the splinter of shell that had bowled him over years before.

" The doctor went down upon his knees. Rapidly examining the bleeding wound, he looked up at me and said grimly, ' This is bad business, Captain, bad business. But he's failed in his undertaking. Nerves must have gone back on him. That was a glancing shot: it didn't penetrate.' He rapidly ran his eye around the room. ' See where it went?' he said, pointing to a ragged break in the plastering.

" We lifted Bob from the floor and laid him on the bed. The doctor went to work and stopped the bleeding, talking softly to me all the while. 'I don't like it at all,' he said. 'He'll not die from this, but I'm in doubt about the effect it'll have on his brain. It's a nasty shock for a man in his over-wrought condition. Queer, isn't it, that I should be patching up the same place that I worked over so long ago? He's in for brain fever, poor devil! It's a hard thing to say, Elliott, but I'm not sure that he wouldn't have been luckier if his lead had gone straight in.'

" Well, the rest of the story can be told in few words. Bob didn't die. The doctors pulled him safely through, and saved a life that might better have been allowed to slip away. For when the fever that followed upon the shock of the wound had burned itself out, the delirium remained, and all that was left of as fine a man as ever served was a hopelessly insane wreck.

" It's twelve years since I've seen him. They wouldn't let me come to visit him at the asylum, fearing that the sight of me might affect him unfavorably. Poor Bob! he's been out of the world for all that time — waiting to wear out! From time to time I've had reports from the doctors, but never a cheering one until to-day, when I received a letter from Bob himself — and by the same mail got word that death had come at last to bring him his release.

"It seems that the end came very suddenly. There was a physical collapse, as if his vital machinery had run down all at once. But at the very last the cloud lifted from his mind, and before he died he had become, mentally, almost his old self. It was on his last afternoon that he dictated this letter to me." The colonel leaned forward and took the envelope from his desk. "I'm going to read you a paragraph or two from it, because it concerns you, in a way."

The colonel glanced at his two listeners. Van Sickles was smoking calmly, as is his wont. Pollard's cigar had gone out, and he was bending forward in his chair, with his eyes expectantly fixed upon the chief. It was evident that he was not a little moved by what he had heard.

"Here's what he says," said the colonel, rapidly glancing through the contents of one sheet, and beginning to read from the second: "'They tell me, Harry, that you've found it impossible to stay out of the service, even in these peaceful times, and that you've a command of your own — that it's fallen to you to be at the head of the regiment that's keeping our old name and number alive. If that's true, I've a favor to ask from you. Don't think it the whim of a madman, for it's not. To come to it at once, I want a major's escort when they put me away. It's my soberly sane desire, and the last one that I shall have in this world. You'll see that I'm not disappointed? I knew you would, and I'll thank you in advance. Perhaps you'd do well to let the boys of the ' Old Regiment ' know when and where the funeral will be : some of them might like to be there. But I'll leave it all to you.' "

The colonel paused. His voice had become just the least bit unsteady. To cover his feelings he struck a match, but forgot to apply it to his cigar until it had burned down so far that he had to drop it hastily upon the floor.

" Is that all, sir ? " asked Pollard, when the colonel stopped reading.

" Perhaps I might give you the last paragraph," replied the chief huskily, again turning to the sheet that he held. " ' Good-bye,

Harry,' it runs. 'I'm tiring fast, and the nurse says I must stop and rest. You'll remember about the escort? I've no family left, and few friends, so I must look to you for everything. We'll meet again sometime, I've a firm conviction. Things will be happier then, and brighter. So good-bye once more, old fellow, and God bless —.'" The colonel choked, and stopped abruptly.

Major Pollard pulled himself up from his chair. "Will you order out my battalion as escort, sir?" he asked earnestly. "I should consider it a great honor, and I'm sure that the men would look at it in the same way."

"I hope you'll find something for me to do," began Van Sickles, coming towards the colonel's desk. "I'd be glad to help in any way; about flowers, or music, or —"

"Thank you both," said the chief, giving a hand to each. "I knew you'd help me out in this. Yes, I'll order you out, Pollard. I'll have the adjutant issue a special order at once. Perhaps you'd do well to speak to your company commanders about it now, before they dismiss. We'll have the funeral on Sunday afternoon. I shall call on you, Van, for help in a number of little matters between now and then."

Pollard left the room, going to pass word to his captains. The colonel and Van Sickles went to the staff-room, where the adjutant and sergeant major were wrestling with the never-ending "paper work" of regimental headquarters.

"Charley," said the chief, as he came to the adjutant's desk, "what was the number of the last regimental special order?"

"I think it was 48, sir," said the adjutant, dragging the order-book from its resting place, and rapidly running over its pages. "Yes, 48 it was."

"Then I'll trouble you to make me out 49," said the colonel. "Have it run something like this: 'The 3rd Battalion will report to Major Pollard, on Sunday next, for the performance of escort duty at the funeral of Robert Hunnewell Sheldon, late major of this regiment when in the service of the United States, 1861–65.'"

It was a bright, warm Sunday. Against the cloudless sky the grim battlements of the armory towered up in bold relief. Upon the

tiny flanking turret which caps one corner of
the massive watch-tower, the half-masted
flag hung down in drooping folds of white
and red, unstirred by any passing breeze.

The streets were almost deserted. But
within the great armory there was unwonted
life and movement: and when the clocks of
the city were striking the hour of three, the
ponderous, iron-bound doors swung heavily
apart, and, company by company, Major Pollard's battalion of The Third came marching
out, under the frowning archway and down
the wide granite steps.

The major formed his command in line,
facing the entrance. A moment later he
brought the battalion to a " present," faced
about, and saluted, as six sergeants of the
regiment came slowly down the steps, bearing out into the June sunlight a plain, black
casket, which they placed in the waiting
hearse.

Then came a handful of men in citizen's
dress, the survivors of the ' Old Regiment '
— grey-haired men, most of them, but all
wearing proudly the bronze star, and the
Maltese cross of their long-disbanded army
corps. These were followed by the colonel

and nearly all the officers of the active regiment, in full dress; for the story had spread
through The Third, and — though the chief
had expressed no formal wish — it somehow
had become understood that he would be glad
to have this mark of respect shown for the
dead officer who had been his friend and
comrade.

The escorting battalion moved to its position, the muffled drums of the field music
began to beat, and the column, leaving the
deserted armory to its Sunday quiet, slowly
took up the march towards the elm-shadowed
churchyard where, beside two low, green
mounds, an open grave lay waiting.

The chaplain, book in hand, took his place
beside the heap of freshly turned mould,
ready to begin the recital of the solemn service for the dead. "Forasmuch as it hath
pleased Almighty God to take unto Himself
the soul of our brother here departed," he
read, slowly and distinctly, as the coffin was
lowered gently to its resting place; "we
therefore commit his body to the ground;
earth to earth, ashes to ashes, dust to dust."

The service ended, and the chaplain softly
closed his book. Then came the commands

for the firing, given in a tone strangely unlike that to which the men were accustomed. Three echoing volleys followed, telling those who chanced to hear that another soldier of the half-forgotten war had been laid at rest.

The blue-white smoke from the rifles, silvered here and there by shafts of sunlight, drifted lazily up through the branches of the overhanging elms: there was an interval of silence, finally broken by the mellow notes of a bugle thrilling out the bars of *Taps*, the soldier's requiem; and then the escort broke into column and marched away, leaving the little knot of older men still standing in the shady churchyard.